Books should be returned or renewed by the last date
above. Renew by phone **08458 247 200** or online
www.kent.gov.uk/libs

A:
3/14

BEATON M.C

BANISHMENT

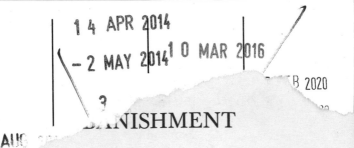

BANISHMENT

The Daughters of Mannerling Series (in order)

BANISHMENT

M. C. Beaton

Canvas

Constable & Robinson Ltd
55–56 Russell Square
London WC1B 4HP
www.constablerobinson.com

First ebook edition published in the United States by
RosettaBooks LLC, New York, 2011

This edition first published in the UK by Canvas,
an imprint of Constable & Robinson Ltd, 2014

A copy of the British Library Cataloguing in
Publication data is available from the British Library

ISBN 978-1-78033-323-6 (A-format paperback)
ISBN 978-1-47211-288-0 (ebook)

1 3 5 7 9 10 8 6 4 2

Typeset by TW Typesetting, Plymouth, Devon

Printed and bound by
CPI Group (UK) Ltd, Croydon, CR0 4YY

CONTENTS

ONE

And behold there was a very stately palace in front of him, the name of which was Beautiful.

JOHN BUNYAN

Everyone who had ever visited Mannerling, home of the Beverley family, declared it to be the most beautiful house in England. It was ornamented with the finest sculptures and paintings and also ornamented by the six daughters of the house, all accounted diamonds of the first water.

But one hot summer's day, as they sprawled around the schoolroom at the top of the house, they seemed for once to have forgotten that they were the fabulous Misses Beverley. For life had held out the promise of a dizzying success for all of them – success for ladies of the Regency meaning suitable marriage. And yet Isabella, the eldest, now nineteen, had just returned from her come-out at the Season unwed. She did not 'take,' much to her parents' and sisters' bewilderment, for Isabella was undoubtedly a flawless beauty. She was tall and statuesque with masses of rich curly brown hair, a straight little nose, and a small,

1

well-shaped mouth. Being chilly and haughty themselves, her parents, Sir William and Lady Beverley, had trained Isabella from childhood to believe that no one was good enough for her and it was that attitude that had kept suitors at bay, even the ones who would have liked a share in the Beverley fortune, all being perfectly sure that any offer of marriage would be rejected.

To her equally haughty and proud sisters it was a mystery, and they had foregathered in the schoolroom to try to find out – tactfully – if Isabella could offer any suggestion as to the reason for her failure. They made a pretty picture. Jessica, at eighteen, rivalled Isabella in beauty with her auburn hair and hazel eyes. Then there were the twins, aged seventeen, Rachel and Abigail, with fairer hair than the rest and very wide blue eyes. After them came Belinda, black-haired, quiet and placid, and then Lizzie, the youngest, red-haired and green-eyed and considered too waiflike to ever aspire to anything like her sisters' beauty but accounted well enough in her way.

Jessica slid into the attack, saying as if idly, 'You have not yet told us of the balls and parties, Isabella. And what of suitors?'

'There were many, both balls, parties, and suitors,' said Isabella with studied vagueness. 'We must go shortly. We are to call at the vicarage.'

'Must we?' asked Lizzie. 'I cannot like Mary.' Mary Stoppard was the vicar's daughter. Sir William and his wife liked to patronize Mr and Mrs Stoppard, who toadied to them quite dreadfully, and so the girls were expected to be civil to Mary, whom they heartily despised. Despite their arrogance, the Beverley sisters had reason to despise Mary. She paid them extravagant compliments with a little smile pinned on her mouth that never quite reached her perpetually watching and calculating black eyes.

'To return to your Season,' went on Jessica with rare persistence, 'I cannot understand why you will not tell us more about it.'

'Well, to be sure,' said Isabella, affecting a yawn, 'it was all quite tedious and exhausting. One dances until dawn.'

'One does that when we have a ball here,' put in Rachel.

But in vain did they try by various ways to get Isabella to tell them anything about her Season. They were worried. They had been brought up to believe that they, the Beverley sisters, were the cream of society and could have their pick of gentlemen.

They dispersed to put on their bonnets and collect gloves and fans and parasols, keeping their lady's-maids running here and there. Then they gathered in the hall, that splendid hall with its high painted ceiling and from which sprang the grand staircase, leading to an upper chain of saloons on the first floor, each one decorated a different colour, each one richly furnished. The Beverleys liked to show off the grandeur of their home, although doubting that anyone in the county could match their Norman lineage other than a duke, but would invite lesser mortals to balls and routs, a double row of footmen dressed in gold-and-red livery lining the staircase. The Beverleys kept a great number of servants and so the girls had grown up never knowing what it was like to dress or undress themselves, open a door for themselves, or even to draw a chair forward to sit down.

In the open carriage, Isabella lowered her parasol and looked up at the great house, Mannerling, as if for comfort. It was a seventeenth-century mansion in warm red brick with two wings on either side, added in the eighteenth century, springing out gracefully from the central building. The gardens around the mansion were a miracle of manicured lawns, vistas, a Greek temple, trees, and flowers. The day was sunny and clear with only the lightest of breezes.

Isabella could not understand her failure herself. She had had private dreams of bringing some earl or duke home with her, watching his face as he first saw Mannerling, of showing off her home, her beloved home. But she had not dreamt of love or kisses. Like her sisters, the only passion she had ever known was for Mannerling.

The sisters lounged in the carriage in graceful attitudes as it moved slowly down the long drive lined on either side with lime trees. Normally, they were contented and at ease with each other. But Isabella's failure and her refusal to talk about it had cast a shadow on them. As they alighted at the vicarage, Isabella had the mortification of hearing one twin whisper to the other, 'Do not press her. Obviously no gentleman wanted her.'

Isabella knew that her younger sisters had always

4

looked up to her. She believed she had lost stature in their eyes, a stature that was further diminished, she felt, by Mary Stoppard's oily attempts at tact.

'Dear Miss Beverley,' she cooed, 'so wonderful to have our brightest star shining amongst us once more. Mrs Turlow was just saying the other day that it was a wonder Miss Beverley had arrived back unengaged, but I quickly put her in her place. "There is no man good enough for our beauty," that's what I said.'

'Can we talk about something else?' demanded Isabella, her normally dulcet tones showing a new edge.

'To be sure, to be sure,' said Mary. 'You are holding the summer ball as usual?'

'Next month,' said Jessica. Isabella suddenly longed to leave the stuffy vicarage and run away, run across the fields and be entirely on her own. But she never ran or made any rapid vulgar movement. She had overheard her parents going through lists of gentlemen to be invited to the ball. 'Surely Isabella will find *someone*,' she had heard her mother wail.

'The invitations have been sent out this age,' said Lizzie. 'Didn't you get yours, Miss Stoppard?'

'Yes, I did, yes, I did,' said Mary. 'But someone was just saying it might be cancelled in view of . . .'

'In view of what?' demanded Jessica.

'Stupid little me,' said Mary, putting a coy finger on the tip of her chin. 'It's the heat. I do not know what I am saying.'

But Isabella suddenly knew that the gossips were no doubt speculating that the Beverleys might cancel the unnecessary expense of a ball when they had already spent so much on a lavish Season to no avail.

'My apologies.' Isabella stood up. 'No, stay,' she said to her sisters. 'I need some air.'

She went outside and walked up to the carriage and threw her parasol and fan into it and then her hat. 'Tell my sisters I will walk,' she announced to the amazed coachman. She walked off down the dusty road under the summer sun and then climbed over a stile into a meadow and then began to run and run, bone-pins scattering from her elaborate Roman hair-style. She felt she was running away from every hot London saloon and ballroom, from every whisper, every speculation. She reached the other side of the meadow and plunged into the green shade of the woods, finally slowing down to a walk and then sinking down on a flat rock which lay beside a lazy little river.

What had gone wrong? She had behaved just as she ought, a model of decorum. At first, at the beginning of the Season, it had been wonderful. Men had stood up in their carriages in Hyde Park to get a better look at her beauty. At the first ball, she had been besieged by partners. She had despised the hurly-burliness of some of the debutantes, who, in her opinion, had flirted disgracefully. Isabella Beverley would not stoop to flirt. Her conversation was always about the beauties of Mannerling. And yet, young Lord Riverdale, who had taken her into supper, had yawned, cut across one of her descriptions of the grand staircase at Mannerling and said, 'I say, look at that quiz of a man over there!' Startled, she had politely followed the direction of his waving quizzing-glass and then had returned to her favourite subject. And he had yawned again! Quite openly and for all to see. And two of the debutantes, quite plain girls, surely not to be considered rivals, had tittered behind their fans. But one of the plain girls had subsequently become engaged to Lord Riverdale before the end of the Season. There was also a feeling that she, Isabella, was a bit of a joke. She thought for one awful moment at a rout towards the end of the Season that she had heard herself called boring. 'Here comes Miss Boring,' a man had said as she had mounted the staircase of a London town house flanked by her parents, but he could not possibly have been referring to *her*. And yet . . . and yet . . . no suitor had come calling. Other girls received bouquets of flowers and poems, but not Isabella.

She knew that her parents were hopeful of puffing her off at the annual summer ball. They had sent an invitation to the Duke of Severnshire but he had sent a polite reply to say he would be otherwise engaged on that evening. The Beverleys had never seen this duke. Sir William and Lady Beverley had even gone so far as to call at his home. His butler had said he was out and yet as they had driven off, Lady Beverley was sure she had seen him looking out of a window. She knew what he looked like, for she had seen a portrait of him, albeit a bad portrait, on display at the local town hall.

The Beverleys had decided that the duke must be a recluse and eccentric at that, for who in the rest of the county did not crave an invitation to Mannerling!

Isabella felt dusty and hot and, leaning down,

cupped some water from the little stream and splashed her hot face.

Then she rose to her feet and began to make her way home across the fields, well aware that the coachman would have reported her strange behaviour to her parents. For a while, as she walked under the summer sun, past fields of wheat turning and shining in the breeze, she felt tired and somehow free. She wondered what it would be like to be Miss Beverley of Nowhere.

And yet, as she finally walked up the long drive and saw the magnificence of her family home spread in front of her, she felt a tug at her heart as if approaching a lover. She realized for the first time that she must look like a guy with her gown all white dust and her hair tumbling about her shoulders. Her lady's-maid, Maria, ran out to meet her, chiding and exclaiming. Then her mother followed her up the staircase, saying in her flat cold voice that the doctor had been sent for. The coachman had reported that Miss Beverley was suffering from a touch of the sun.

In vain did Isabella protest. She was firmly put to bed, a towel soaked in cologne was placed on her forehead, and then the doctor came and prescribed a purge. Isabella waited until he had left, dismissed her maid, and poured the mixture out of the window. She had endured this doctor's purges before and did not want another.

She tried to insist later that she was well enough to rise for dinner, but the Beverleys, that is, mother, father and sisters, were too shocked by her behaviour

8

to risk more of it and so she had to content herself with invalid food on a tray in her room.

By next day Isabella, looking back on her own behaviour, came to believe that she had indeed had a touch of the sun. Restored once more to elegant beauty, exquisitely gowned and coiffed, walking through the elegant rooms of her home, under the painted ceilings where gods and goddesses disported themselves in a way that meant nothing to the virginal Isabella, she felt once more in her proper place and at peace with herself. Was it her fault that she was too good and too beautiful for any man in London? There must have been a poor crop at the Season. She had been unlucky, that was all.

In the time leading up to the ball, Sir William was increasingly absent from home, saying he had pressing business matters to attend to in London. But these were masculine things, surely, and of little interest to the daughters of Mannerling, who discussed endlessly what they would wear and how the rooms should be decorated.

Lady Beverley had never concerned herself with such vulgar matters as the price of anything. Swathes of silk to decorate the walls of the saloons were ordered from the mercers of Ludgate Hill, and new gowns for her daughters from the finest dressmaker; Gunter, the confectioner, was to be brought all the way from London at great expense to cater for the guests; and Neil Gow and his band, who played at Almack's during the Season, were hired to entertain the guests.

After a discreet lapse of time, the bills for all this splendour would come flooding in, to be coped with by Sir William's secretary, James Ducket. Extra servants were hired for the great evening, although Mannerling already had a large staff. As a last extravagance, Lady Beverley had ordered new livery for the footmen and gold dress swords to ornament them further.

Although the Beverley sisters did not work at all to help with the preparations – such a thought never entered their heads – they all confessed wearily that they would be glad when the great night arrived, for so much bustle and fuss was exhausting.

And yet it was Isabella who began to feel slightly uneasy about all the expense, particularly when she found a few days before the ball that her mother had ordered all the bed hangings to be changed for new ones. Now that she had attended balls and parties in great houses, she knew that even the grandest did not go on in such a lavish style, with the possible exception of the Prince Regent.

The sisters were to be gowned in various pastel shades of muslin. It was unfashionable for young ladies to wear expensive jewels, a simple strand of pearls or a coral necklace being the fashion. But Sir William liked to see his daughters bedecked and glittering with the finest jewels, although Isabella had conformed to fashion while in London.

The sisters bent their heads over the guest list, groaning a little over familiar names of gentlemen. That one lisped, this one was too poor, that one was too old, until they came to a late entry, Viscount

Fitzpatrick. Mr Ducket, the secretary, was pressed for details. Lord Fitzpatrick, he said, was an Irish peer who had recently bought a property in Severnshire. 'Oh, an *Irish* peer,' they said in dismay, Irish peers being not bon ton, and dismissed the viscount from their minds.

The evening of the ball arrived. Isabella wondered what had happened to her as she stood at the top of the grand staircase with her parents. Her poise and equanimity were slowly deserting her again. Sir William had returned from London only that day and he appeared to have aged, but he stood with his wife and daughters and smiled and bowed as he greeted the guests. When Isabella finally moved into the 'ball-room,' which had been made from the chain of saloons, she realized that the mysterious Irish viscount had not put in an appearance. Her hand was instantly claimed for a dance by a Mr Tulley, who was not handsome at all and whose property was reputed to be falling into rack and ruin. Isabella stifled a sigh. The diamond tiara, which she had not worn in London, once more ornamented her hair, and a heavy diamond necklace, her neck. She had a brief little memory of what it had been like to run free across the fields but quickly banished it. Such thoughts were treacherous. She was the eldest sister and must set an example to the others. What of? 'Failure,' jeered a nasty new little niggling voice in her brain.

At the end of the dance, her father introduced her to Viscount Fitzpatrick. The viscount had just arrived. Isabella sank into an elegant curtsy – but not too low.

11

One must remember he was an Irish peer. He was a tall man. It was not often Isabella had to look up to anyone in this age of short people, but the Irishman topped her by a head. He was impeccably dressed and he had well-coiffed thick black hair worn in the Windswept, but his blue eyes in his lightly tanned face were bright, intelligent, and mocking, almost as if he found the Beverleys and their ball a prime joke. Sir William and Lady Beverley exchanged glances and then went off, leaving the couple together. Isabella's heart sank. From formerly being considered fit partner only for a duke, her parents might now have lowered their sights and thought an Irish peer good enough.

'You are a beautiful ornament to a beautiful home,' said the viscount.

'I am very proud of my home.' Isabella sounded complacent. 'And my sisters,' she added, smiling indulgently across the room to where the other five stood in conversation.

'It's like a museum,' he said in awe, 'and you and your sisters are like exhibits under glass.'

Her eyes flashed with anger. 'That is impertinent.'

'I am allowed an observation,' he said with unimpaired good humour. 'Pray walk with me and show me some of the beauties of your home.'

So Isabella led him back to the landing overlooking the main staircase and pointed out with pride the painted ceiling, a swirling baroque assembly of classical deities, and then her voice gained energy and warmth as she went on to describe some of the many treasures of the house: the remarkable walnut

Queen Anne chairs in the drawing room; the delicately carved rococo chimney-piece and overmantel of the fireplace in the library; the chinoiserie mirrors in the Blue Saloon; the large musical clock in the Red Saloon, which played a different tune for every day of the week; and the two Boulle marriage chests in the morning room.

He gave a little shiver and his blue eyes danced. 'Faith, it's like being at an auction sale,' he said.

'I *beg* your pardon, my lord.'

'It's the way you give me an inventory of the contents. I am a superstitious man and would feel it was tempting fate if I itemized the contents of my home to a guest. "How much am I bid for this fine painting?" – that sort of thing. Now shall we dance?'

Isabella was tempted to snub him as she had snubbed so many in London but was taken aback when he said gently, 'That is, if it is correct to ask a married lady such as yourself to dance.'

'You jest. I am not married.'

'Oh, but you are.' He drew her arm through his own and led her back into the ballroom. 'You are married to this house, to Mannerling. Such devotion, such passion is wasted on bricks and mortar and geegaws.'

She opened her mouth to protest but he drew her into the steps of a waltz. He chatted easily about his problems of getting his English estate in order and she began to relax. There was a warmth and friendliness about him that she found engaging. She liked to pigeon-hole people and so she put him down in her mind as an amusing rattle, not marriageable but

13

entertaining, and in relaxing in his company and laughing at his sallies did not realize that animation was adding to her beauty.

He danced again with her that evening and after it was over led her up to her father and asked permission to go out riding with her. Lady Beverley, standing beside her husband, said, to Isabella's embarrassment, 'We expect our daughter to marry the highest in the land.'

'But of course,' said Lord Fitzpatrick easily, seeming not in the least put out. 'Shall I call for you, say, at two o'clock on Monday, Miss Isabella?'

'Thank you,' said Isabella. She could not quite believe that her stately and elegant mother had been so, well, blunt.

The ball proceeded to its elegant end. Guests who were staying went off to their respective rooms, guests who were leaving got into their carriages and bowled off down the long drive.

Isabella was glad to retire to her room and allow her sleepy maid to prepare her for bed. Most ladies chatted after a ball to their servants, but not Isabella. She had been surrounded by so many servants since the day she was born and considered them part of the furniture; and besides, had been influenced by a father who expected all servants to be seen and not heard and even to turn their faces to the wall as he passed. To her surprise there was a scratching at the door. She sent her maid to answer it, thinking it might be one of her sisters come for a chat, but it was a tired and worried Mr Ducket, the secretary, who walked into the room.

'I crave your pardon for disturbing you so late, Miss Isabella,' he said, 'but Sir William is leaving directly for London and wishes to take all the jewels to be cleaned.'

Isabella looked at her tiara and necklace, still lying on the toilet-table where the maid had placed them when she had taken them off. 'They were cleaned before the beginning of the Season, if you remember,' she said. 'Pray leave them.'

'Sir William is anxious to depart and was most insistent that I collect all the jewels.'

'Oh, very well,' said Isabella.

Mr Ducket snapped his fingers. Two footmen entered carrying a large iron-bound box. They threw back the lid and Mr Ducket put the tiara and necklace into it.

'And all the others,' he said apologetically.

Isabella felt too tired to question him further. She nodded to her maid, who went to fetch Isabella's jewel box. The contents were added to those in the chest.

But when they had gone, when a weary Isabella climbed into bed, a bright image of the jewels in the chest came into her mind. She remembered seeing Jessica's ruby necklace, the twins' pearl sets, bit and pieces of her mother's collection poking up amongst the others. How odd that her father should decide to get them all cleaned at once.

The sisters all felt rather flat and low after the excitement of the ball. They talked of beaux but without much enthusiasm. Isabella's invitation to go riding with the viscount did not interest them. The Beverleys did not judge men by looks and character but by fortune and rank. But Isabella found herself actually looking forward to the outing. It was all very safe. He knew the Beverleys considered him unmarriageable. The Beverleys were of higher rank because of lineage and wealth and they were *English*.

On the Monday when Isabella went out with the viscount she was mounted on a placid white mare with a broad back.

'That must be like riding on a sofa,' he commented, looking down at her from the height of his stallion. 'Do you never wish to ride something speedier?'

Isabella patted the mare's neck. 'I thought we could ride about the grounds and I could show you some of the features of our estate.'

'And I think we should ride to my place where I can find you a mount and then we can go for a proper ride.'

As he said this, they had ridden a certain distance from Mannerling and it was almost as if the spell the house normally cast on her was losing its hold as Isabella said, 'Are you so sure, my lord, that I can ride anything more exciting?'

'I think you would tell me you could not.'

'Very well. But is it conventional to go to your estate?'

'My aunt is in residence. We shall be going to the stables, perhaps to the house later.'

'Then we will see whether I can manage your choice of mount.'

Isabella was wearing a pale-blue velvet riding dress frogged with gold. On her head was a jaunty little hat with a chiffon scarf wound round it, the ends being left to float out from the back. He was in a well-cut black jacket, doeskin breeches, and boots with brown tops.

They rode away from the Mannerling estate at a sedate canter, which was all Isabella's mare could manage. As they approached the stables of Perival, the name of Lord Fitzpatrick's estate, Isabella began to look curiously about her. There seemed to be a great deal of activity everywhere. Men were working on the roofs of cottages, men and women were working in the fields. She had expected everything to be run down and so it was, but energetic efforts appeared to be underway to put everything right.

'I bought it cheaply,' he said as if reading her thoughts, 'although the repairs and work to be put in on the fields will come to quite a bit.'

She wanted to say that she thought Irish peers never had any money at all but did not because it would be impolite. When they arrived at the stables, she had a clear view of the house, a fairly modern mansion; she remembered hearing that it had been built in 1750. It was solid and square without ornament or even creeper to soften its lines, but it looked sturdy and well-built.

The viscount had brought servants from Ireland, particularly stable staff, and he was amused at the effect on them of the beauty of Isabella Beverley. His head groom stood open-mouthed and had to be gently called to order. A tall, rangy-looking hunter

17

was brought out for Isabella's inspection. 'His name is Satan,' said the viscount. 'Do you think you can handle him?'

The pride of the Beverleys came to Isabella's rescue. 'Of course,' she said haughtily.

Her side-saddle was taken off the mare and put on the hunter, which was led out to the mounting-block. She was helped up into the saddle. The ground seemed an awful long way below her. 'Ready?' asked the viscount and she nodded.

They set off and then the viscount turned off down a bridle-path lined with trees. 'Now,' he said, 'let's see how fast we can go.'

Her heart in her mouth, Isabella spurred Satan to a gallop. He went off like the wind. At first it was terrifying, then it was exhilarating, then she felt like singing for joy as the great horse flew like a bird straight down the path and then across open fields. She finally reined in beside the viscount at the top of a rise, her eyes shining and her face flushed. 'Well done, Miss Beverley,' he said with a touch of surprise in his voice.

'You play a dangerous game, my lord,' she said lightly. 'What would you have done had I not been able to handle the brute?'

'You forget, I am an Irishman. I could tell by the very way you sat on Satan as we rode out from the stables that you could hold him. Besides, he's safe enough. Neither a biter nor a bolter.'

'I would like to buy him,' said Isabella.

'My regrets, lady, he is not for sale.'

'I would give you a good price.'

'That is one of my favourite horses and I would not part with him for money . . . or for love.' His blue eyes glinted at her. 'Anyway, there are things that are not for sale, O rich Miss Beverley.'

'Such as?'

'Such as warmth and loyalty and friendship. Most of my servants would opt to work for me without wages should I fall on hard times.'

'As would ours, I hope,' said Isabella.

'Would they now? Care for them, do you? Look after them when they're sick?'

'We have an excellent butler and housekeeper. The welfare of the servants is their business.'

'I have heard it said in the county that Sir William expects the servants to make themselves scarce when he approaches, or to turn their faces to the wall. You know, that sort of master does not often command loyalty, and one never knows when one will need loyalty.'

'My father is a fair master and pays the wages promptly each quarter-day.'

'Money again. I fear you love only material things, Miss Beverley. Your soul is made up of bricks and mortar and money – oh, and woods and trees, too, if carefully domesticated and put into pleasing vistas.'

'Really, my lord, I wonder you care for my company as you are so highly critical of me!'

'You forget your exceptional beauty.'

'I am tired,' said Isabella abruptly, 'and wish to return.'

'We shall take tea with my aunt first. She will enjoy your company.'

'Perhaps another time . . .'

'I told her to expect you, and old ladies are not to be disappointed.'

And so Isabella, after they had returned to the stables and dismounted, found herself meekly accompanying him into his home.

She was pleased, for she had taken him in dislike because of his criticisms, to notice that his house was not particularly richly furnished. In the drawing room the paintings were all dark hunting scenes or landscapes, badly in need of cleaning. It was then that she remembered her father taking all the jewels to London. How very odd. But then her attention was taken by a small square lady with a round red face who had risen to meet her. 'Aunt, may I present Miss Beverley, our neighbour,' said the viscount. 'Miss Beverley, my Aunt Mary, Mrs Kennedy.'

'Sure and it's the beauty you are,' said Mrs Kennedy, beaming up at Isabella. 'Come sit yourself down and give me your crack.'

How terribly vulgar she is, thought Isabella, feeling more superior by the minute. She sat next to Mrs Kennedy on the sofa and accepted a cup of tea. Mrs Kennedy blew noisily on her tea before drinking it with noisy slurps.

'Ah, that's better, sure it is,' she said with a sigh. 'Nothing like a dish of tay. Did you enjoy your ride, Miss Beverley.'

'Yes, I thank you, ma'am.'

'And try the fruit-cake, do. I made it meself wit' me own hands. Do you bake, Miss Beverley?'

Isabella gave a little laugh. 'I leave such things to the servants, Mrs Kennedy.'

'Ah, but to be a good mistress you should be able to do everything your servants can do and better. Is that not the truth now, Guy?'

'Not this generation, Aunt Mary,' said the viscount. 'You are sadly out of touch with fashionable ladies. A fashionable lady never even opens the door for herself.'

'Now that's a crying shame,' said Mrs Kennedy.

'I see no reason for an unnecessary training in house-keeping,' said Isabella firmly.

'You might not always have servants . . .' began Mrs Kennedy, and to Isabella's surprise the old lady promptly fell silent after a warning look from her nephew. But the viscount had surely warned his aunt that she was in danger of being impertinent. Isabella began to talk easily about the ball at Mannerling, of the courses served at supper, of the music, of how everyone had fallen in love with Mannerling.

'There are six of you,' said Mrs Kennedy. 'The six beautiful daughters of Mannerling. Did nobody fall in love with any of you? Or was the love all for the house?'

God spare me from the Irish, thought Isabella, feeling cross again. She rose to her feet and said, 'I really must leave. My sisters and mother will be wondering what has become of me.'

'Then you must call again, m'dear,' said Mrs Kennedy warmly. 'You know the way.'

Her mare was once more saddled up and she and the viscount made their staid way to Mannerling. He again pointed out various repairs that were taking place, and how he planned to drain the six acre, idle, harmless country chit-chat which made Isabella feel quite in charity with him.

She made her goodbyes. He refused her polite invitation to step indoors for some refreshment. He bowed, said he would call on her quite soon, and swung his athletic body up into the saddle.

Isabella went to join her sisters and mother in the drawing room. She gave a very funny description of Mrs Kennedy which set them all laughing, and wondered why she began to feel quite small and mean and diminished.

She changed the subject abruptly by asking, 'Why did Papa find it necessary to take all the jewellery to London to be cleaned, Mama? Most of mine was cleaned before the beginning of the Season.'

'I really don't know, my dear,' said Lady Beverley. 'But be sure your father knows what he is doing.'

Later that day, Isabella went to the study where the secretary was working over some estate papers. 'Mr Ducket,' she said, 'that mare of mine is a trifle tame. I wish to buy a horse with more speed and power.'

To her surprise he looked awkward and embarrassed. 'It is not for me to say, Miss Beverley, whether you should have a new horse or not. I beg you to apply to Sir William when he returns.'

'But that is not necessary,' said Isabella. 'I do not know any horse dealers. I wish you to arrange it. Have a selection of horses brought to the stables for my inspection.'

'I must insist that you wait for your father's return, Miss Beverley.'

'I find your attitude most odd, Mr Ducket. We have always applied to you in the past for things when Papa has been absent.'

'I am sorry, but those are my instructions,' he said.

'From Papa? How strange,' said Isabella huffily. 'I am sure you are mistaken and he will be most cross with you on his return.'

She felt quite taken aback. She had never been refused anything before.

TWO

Eating the bitter bread of banishment

WILLIAM SHAKESPEARE

Any lady of less arrogance and pride than Isabella Beverley would have thought often of the handsome viscount, but as a week went past, Isabella almost forgot about him, until on the following Monday he sent a footman over with a request that she should go out on a drive with him. The weather during the preceding week had been rainy and unseasonably cold, but the sun had started to shine again and Isabella, after consulting her mother, decided that a further acquaintance with the viscount could be used to advantage. 'Perhaps I have been too stiff and cold with the gentlemen I have met,' said Isabella earnestly. 'I could practise my social manners on this viscount.'

And so, attired in a carriage gown and smart hat, Isabella smiled at the viscount as he assisted her into his curricle and called to the Mannerling groom to stand away from the horses' heads.

'Where are we going?' asked Isabella. She did hope they were not going to visit his aunt.

24

'To Hedgefield.'

'To the town? But there is a fair on today, is there not?'

'Do you not like fairs?'

'I have only been to one. Are they not rather noisy and vulgar?'

'Great fun, I assure you, Miss Beverley.'

Isabella thought that if she protested, then he might decide to take her to see his aunt. So she gave a little smile and said it might be amusing.

He reached a crossroads where dead and rotting bodies swung over their heads on a gibbet and then took the left turn, which led to the town of Hedgefield.

As they entered the town, Isabella began to wish she had stated firmly that she did not want to go. So many people, so many *common* people, so many booths and flags and bunting, so much noise. She felt the quiet, cool rooms of Mannerling calling her home, calling her back.

He drove into the yard of the central inn, the Green Man. 'Would you like some refreshment first?' he asked as he helped her down and then threw a coin to an ostler who had come to take the horses to the stables.

But Isabella shook her head. A few moments at the fair and then she would plead a headache and ask to be taken home. They left the inn-yard and began to move among the booths, Isabella holding in her skirts, as if brushing them against the common herd would contaminate her in some way.

'This conjuror is very good,' said the viscount,

stopping outside a booth. To Isabella's horror, he bought two tickets and ushered her into the greenish gloom of the tent behind.

I shall *never* forgive him for this, thought Isabella as she sat on a hard bench at the very front. The fact that everyone was exclaiming and staring at her beauty went unnoticed by her. For all her faults, she was not vain about her looks and assumed everyone was staring at her because she was a stranger and because of the richness of her clothes. A large farmer's wife carrying a basket sat down next to her, children were running and screaming around and under the benches, and the air was full of the smell of oranges, which some of the audience had bought from a seller outside.

Isabella had just decided to feign a headache and ask to be taken home when the conjuror appeared. He seemed a nervous young man and he was wearing a plain black morning coat and knee-breeches and a high cravat. He looked sadly round the audience and then solemnly appeared to take a coloured ball out of his ear. He looked at it in comic surprise. Then he took another from the back of his neck and another materialized from the top of his head, and so he went on until he had eight small coloured balls which he proceeded to juggle. Then he gave a little sigh and threw them all up in the air . . . and they magically disappeared.

And from that moment, Miss Isabella Beverley promptly forgot her surroundings and sat, fascinated, on the edge of the bench. When he finished his act by producing a whole bowl of live goldfish from under the tails of his coat, she clapped as loudly and rapturously as anyone else. And somehow, as they emerged blinking into the sunlight, Isabella became part of the fair, part of the crowds. She demanded to see the two-headed pig, the Morality play, and the painted lady. She searched through the booths which sold scarves, trinkets, and fans, cakes and jam, exclaiming at how inexpensive everything was, which surprised the viscount, who was amazed to learn that she knew the price of anything.

It was when they were drinking lemonade in the inn that a shadow began to fall across Isabella's bright day. She said, 'My ride on your Satan has quite spoiled me for my quiet mare. Papa is in London. I asked our secretary to see about purchasing me a proper mount and he said I must wait for Papa's return.'

'That seems sensible,' remarked the viscount.

'But Mr Ducket, that's the secretary, has always handled things like that in Papa's absence.'

'A good hunter like Satan costs quite a deal of money. Have you considered that?'

Isabella gave him an amused smile. 'That is one of the problems the Beverley family does not have, my lord.'

He put down his glass and looked at her seriously. 'Things in life can change. Even families as rich as yours can come upon hard times.'

'What can you mean? Such an idea is unthinkable.'

'Just a word of caution. In any case, why worry? You can send a servant over to collect Satan and go for a ride any time you want.'

'Thank you,' said Isabella. 'But it was most odd of you to hint that something might happen to our fortunes. You were hinting, were you not?'

But he appeared not to hear her. 'If we leave now,' he said, 'we can avoid the crush of carriages on the road when the fair finishes.'

She suddenly wanted to tell him about those jewels. But he might voice the worry that had been growing and growing in her mind – that Papa meant to sell them, that something had happened to her golden world. But then the thought that he might confirm her worry in some way frightened her even more. Papa would be back soon and all would be well again.

As they approached Mannerling, the sky had darkened, threatening rain. The house reached out to welcome her. The viscount no longer appeared a charming and handsome companion but a man who was not quite a suitable consort for one of the Beverley sisters.

They rolled past the stables. 'Papa's carriage is there,' exclaimed Isabella. 'It will be so good to see him.'

Again she thanked him and again he refused her offer of refreshment, touching his curly-brimmed beaver and driving off. A rumble of thunder sounded as Isabella went into the mansion.

'Miss Isabella,' said the butler, his face a white disk in the gloom of the hall, 'Sir William is returned and requested that you should join the family in the drawing room.'

The thunder rumbled again. The storm was drawing closer.

Isabella's maid, Maria, had appeared at her elbow quietly, in the way of a good servant, and took her mistress's fan, bonnet, and parasol. As Isabella mounted the stairs, something suddenly made her turn and look back, look down at the hall.

Maria was standing there, on the black and white tiles, as still as a chess piece, and in her eyes was an avid, gloating look which was banished immediately when she saw her mistress looking at her. She bobbed a curtsy and hurried off. Isabella turned and continued to mount the staircase. A bright flash of lightning stabbed through the cupola above her head and then there was a crash of thunder which seemed to rock the house to its very foundations. She shivered in the increasing gloom. Two footmen at the top of the stairs turned and walked in front of her and then threw open the double doors of the drawing room.

She was never to forget the sight that met her eyes. Her father was standing by the fireplace, leaning one arm on the marble mantel and staring down into the black depths of the empty hearth; her mother was weeping quietly; and her sisters, Jessica, Rachel, Abigail, Belinda, and Lizzie, were still and white, as if frozen.

The footmen retired. 'Papa,' said Isabella, 'what has happened?'

Lady Beverley found her voice. 'We are *ruined*,' she wailed.

Isabella felt for a chair and sat down. For once, there was no waiting footman to slide it under her.

'The jewels,' she said. 'What about the jewels? They must have been worth a king's ransom.'

The door opened and Mr Ducket came in. Sir William raised his head and looked wearily at his secretary. 'I have had enough. You tell her.'

He held out his arm to his wife and they supported each other from the room.

Another blinding flash of lightning lit up the white faces of the Beverley sisters. It was followed by a roll of thunder, but slightly fainter than the last. The storm was moving away.

Mr Ducket stood in front of them. He was a plain and neat young man with a precise, unemotional voice. He began to tell them the dreadful facts. Sir William had been gambling and then speculating in risky ventures to try to recoup the money he had lost, and then gambling again. He had finally lost it all. He had lost the money from the sale of the jewels, and in one last dreadful night of gambling in St James's, he had wagered the house and the estates. The winner was a Mr Judd.

Isabella was the first to find her voice. 'Mannerling? Do you mean we shall have to leave Mannerling?'

'Almost immediately.'

'But where shall we live?'

'Brookfield House is vacant.'

Brookfield House had been vacant for some time. It lay on the outskirts of Hedgefield. It had an acre and a half of garden, but no rolling lawns or vistas or woods or farms.

'Brookfield House is *poky*,' moaned Jessica.

'I am afraid Brookfield House is all that the Beverleys can now afford,' said Mr Ducket.

'How could Papa do this to us?' demanded Isabella fiercely.

'In this gambling age, I am afraid great losses are all too common,' said Mr Ducket.

Belinda found her voice. 'But where will the servants live at Brookfield House? Where will you live, Mr Ducket?'

'I already have another position to go to,' he said in his dry way. 'I made provision for this eventuality. As to the other servants, Sir William must decide on the few who are willing to accompany the family.'

'The *few?*' exclaimed Isabella. 'What of our lady's-maids?'

'As to that, I think you will find lady's-maids to be now an unnecessary luxury. If you will all be so good as to excuse me. I have Sir William's affairs to wind up.'

'Stay!' cried Isabella. 'When do we have to leave Mannerling?'

Far away now the thunder rumbled and a watery shaft of sunlight shone in through the long windows.

'In a week's time.'

'A week! But that is not enough time. Good heavens, there are all the art treasures to be boxed up – the paintings, the statuary.'

'Unfortunately,' said Mr Ducket with his hand on the doorknob, 'they are no longer the concern of the Beverleys. Sir William has not only gambled away Mannerling but the contents.'

He left and quietly closed the doors behind him.

* * *

31

During the miserable week that followed, Isabella thought often about the viscount's remarks about loyal servants. The servants of Mannerling seemed almost thrilled at the ruin of the family which they had served. There was a dumb insolence about them, a gloating air. They had been treated like machines and now saw no reason to share in the misery of their betters. Rather, they rejoiced in it.

The sisters wandered through the elegant rooms like wraiths, touching loved treasures with hands that had never known work, gazing out at the elegant vistas which would so very soon be no longer theirs to look on.

None of them had been to Brookfield House. They did not want to know about the place. Sir William and Mr Ducket came and went, with the fourgon piled high with baggage, although the luggage was mostly clothes and such household items they felt could be decently taken away. Even the horses in the stables were to belong to this Mr Judd, this villain, this criminal who had so callously taken their inheritance away.

During that dreadful week the viscount called, but Isabella refused to see him. She now believed he had known of their impending ruin and felt that he might have warned her.

And no one called. For the news of the fall of the Beverleys had spread like wildfire throughout the county. They had patronized and snubbed so many that their ruin was greeted only with a gleeful, gossipy excitement.

Then there were the lawyers and the duns down

from London, closeted in the study for hours at a time, and Sir William would emerge from these sessions stooped and aged.

Mr Ducket, at last driven to pity for the plight of his soon-to-be late employer, wrote to his new employer begging a further few weeks and rented a room at the inn in Hedgefield so that he could continue to wind up Sir William's complicated debts and affairs.

And so the day came quickly when they had to leave Mannerling, being driven for the last time in the family's travelling carriages, for they, too, must be returned to the stables to await the arrival of the new owner. The sisters had cried until they could cry no more. Huddled together, they stared bleakly straight ahead as they bowled down the long drive. The servants were all staying on in the hope of serving Mr Judd, the new owner. New servants had been hired for them from Hedgefield: a cook-housekeeper, four maids, a pot-boy, and an odd man. There was not even a coachman, and certainly not a butler or any footmen.

The sisters sat in silence on the road to Brookfield House. They had grown up each with her own handsome room and lady's-maid. Now they were to share bedrooms and learn to dress themselves and arrange their own hair.

As last the carriage rolled up the weedy drive of Brookfield House, a large square grey building covered in ivy which fluttered and turned in an unseasonably chilly wind.

The new odd man, a stout, cheerful countryman

called Barry Wort, was waiting to collect the last of their belongings from the carriage.

Lady Williams, said a little maid with rosy cheeks and a shy smile, was lying down. She would show the young ladies to their rooms. 'Thank you,' said Isabella, giving the girl a smile. She who had never thanked a servant for anything in her life had decided it was time she began. 'What is your name?'

'Betty, miss.'

'Then lead the way, Betty.'

Oh, the misery of that dark square undistinguished hall, the poky narrow wooden staircase, and the bedrooms, one for Isabella and Jessica, one for the twins, and the other for Belinda and Lizzie.

'Well,' said Isabella to Jessica, 'here we are.'

'Just look at the carpet,' said Jessica. 'It's *worn*.'

'Quite a number of people do not have carpets in the bedrooms, only bare boards. Oh, dear, they must have taken this furniture with the house. The bed hangings will need to come down and be cleaned. I fear, Jessica, that we are going to have to learn about housework after all.'

'Who will teach us? 'Twould be demeaning to ask the servants.'

'Viscount Fitzpatrick's aunt, Mrs Kennedy, would be delighted to help us.'

'That peasant woman! You said she was as common as the barber's chair.'

A painful blush rose up Isabella's cheeks. 'Do not remind me of that. Has it ever occurred to you, Jessica, that we have been most badly brought up?'

'We were brought up as befitted our station,' said Jessica stoutly.

'I do not think so.' Isabella opened the window and let in a gust of cold damp air and looked down at the scrubby garden and balding lawn. She swung round. 'Perhaps had our servants at Mannerling been treated by us as people rather than as machines, we might have been able to command a certain loyalty when disaster struck us. But, no, not us. Not the famous Beverleys.'

'Really, Isabella. You are beginning to talk like a Whig!'

'Perhaps. Losing Mannerling is like a death. We must learn to live with our grief. There is no hope we will ever get our home back. We must make the best of things here. I do not think Mama even knows how to train maids.'

'The cook-housekeeper will do that.'

'Mayhap. Let's explore the rest of our new home.'

There was a dining room off one side of the hall and a drawing room off the other. A long dark passage led to the kitchen at the back and to a cloakroom, study, and parlour. On the first floor were six bedrooms, the sisters in three, Sir William and Lady Beverley in two, and one left spare for a guest. The attics were for the servants.

At the back of the house were several outbuildings and a privy, a small carriage house, and stabling for a mere two horses.

Their first meal in their new home was a disaster. The untrained maids clattered noisily about with the dishes, the port had not been decanted, and the food!

Beverley palates accustomed to the best French cuisine tasted with dismay dry meat, lumpy gravy, and watery vegetables.

'This will not do, Mama,' said Isabella, putting down her knife and fork. 'Who is this cook-housekeeper, and how did we come by her?'

'I do not know, my dear,' said Lady Beverley wanly. 'I do not concern myself with such things. Mr Ducket had to engage servants from the town at the last moment and it is hard to get qualified servants at a moment's notice.'

'Then, if we have to make do with what we have, she will need to be trained.'

'By whom?' wailed Lady Beverley. 'Mrs Pearce is quite a rough woman and will brook no interference in the kitchen.'

'We will see about that,' said Isabella. She found it hard to even look at her father, he who had ruined their lives with his silly gambling. He was drunk, she noticed, not jolly or rowdy, but almost as if drugged, sitting gazing vacantly into space with a fixed smile on his lips.

After dinner she wrote a letter to Mrs Kennedy, saying she would call on her the following afternoon, and then went in search of the odd man. She found him in one of the outbuildings, chopping logs.

'Weather's turned uncommon sharp, Miss Isabella,' said Barry. 'Best to be prepared.'

Isabella gave him a shilling and the letter. 'Would you be so good as to deliver that to Mrs Kennedy at Perival?'

'Certainly.'

'I shall call on her tomorrow.' Isabella looked at Barry in sudden dismay. 'Oh, dear, no carriage, no horses. How do I get there?'

'I could ask them to send a carriage for you, miss.'

'Alas, things that seemed so easy to command before now seem like an imposition. Is there any way I could get there?'

'You could walk, miss, and if you get permission from Sir William, I will act as footman and walk with you.' Isabella's face cleared. 'That would be splendid. Thank you, Barry. We set out about noon.'

'Right, miss. I'll go to deliver this letter direct.'

He touched his forehead and Isabella walked away feeling strangely comforted. It was only as she fell asleep beside Jessica that night that her last waking thought was that her route to Perival would take her past the gates of Mannerling.

Sir William and Lady Beverley were still too cast down by their changed circumstances to raise any objection to their daughter's statement that she was going to call on the viscount's aunt.

Isabella, who appeared to have lost a layer of self-ishness, could not help noticing that they took Mr Ducket's work as their due. She doubted if they had even thanked the man for delaying starting his new employment in order to help them. Isabella had found a simple morning gown and pelisse and a pair of half-boots for her expedition. She was glad the weather had turned fine, but not too warm.

37

She basked a little in her sisters' awed admiration before she set out. Walking! Dear heavens!

Barry was waiting for her, already to Isabella a sturdy and reassuring figure.

They set out along the road, Barry walking a few paces behind, a stout cudgel in his hand in case any footpads should venture out in the daylight to accost them.

There were fresh bodies on the gibbet at the crossroads that day. Isabella averted her eyes.

After another mile, she said, 'Pray walk with me, Barry. I become weary of my own company.'

He fell into step beside her. 'I trust you are not over-fatigued, miss.'

'I am a trifle tired, I must admit, but we are nearly at Mannerling.'

'Yes, miss. As to that, I know another road which will get us to Perival just as quick and yet avoid going near Mannerling.'

'Why should we do that?'

'I thought it might be painful for you, miss, in the circumstances.'

She stopped and looked at him in surprise, noticing the concern in his eyes. 'How kind of you,' she said in a choked voice. 'How very kind. But I would like a look, you know, just down the drive.'

'Very well, miss. Let it be as you wish. But sometimes, I reckon, one has to let go of things.'

The next bend of the road took them to the great iron gates of Mannerling. Barry stood back as Isabella walked slowly up to the closed gates and leaned against them, staring hungrily down the long straight drive to the home which had so recently been her family's.

She gave a choked little sob and turned away.

'Come along, miss,' urged Barry. 'Come away. 'Twon't be long now. A dish of tea will set you to rights.'

Mrs Kennedy looked out of the window of her drawing room and let out a loud squawk of dismay.

'What's amiss?' asked the viscount.

'Fan me ye winds,' she cried, 'if it isn't that poor lamb come all the way here on foot and with only a rough country fellow to escort her.'

With surprising speed in such a plump lady, she hurtled out of the drawing room, down the stairs, out of the front drive and ran to meet Isabella, gathering the startled girl in her arms and giving her a warm hug.

'There now,' said Mrs Kennedy. 'You must be so tired. You should have asked us to send a carriage.'

'I enjoyed the walk,' said Isabella, gently disengaging herself. 'Besides, I had Barry here to protect me.'

Mrs Kennedy looked at the squat burly figure of Barry. 'You're an odd fellow for a footman.'

'Barry Wort at your service,' he said, giving a low bow. 'I am odd man to the Beverley family, being recently engaged.'

Of course the poor Beverleys could no longer afford footmen, thought Mrs Kennedy, leading Isabella towards the house. She turned to Barry on the doorstep. 'If you go to the kitchens, my man, you will find a good jug of ale.'

The viscount came down the stairs to meet them.

For the first time Isabella really took in the fact that he was an extremely handsome man. It was such a pity he was Irish.

In the drawing room, the viscount and his aunt confined their conversation to polite generalities about the weather, crops, and the general state of the nation.

At last Mrs Kennedy asked how Isabella was settling down in her new home.

Isabella, who had had a temporary setback in that her old pride had reasserted itself, remembered the purpose of her visit and that she could not afford pride any more.

'We are experiencing certain difficulties,' she said, 'because of the speed with which we had to set up house at Brookfield. The servants, such as we have, are untrained, and the cook-housekeeper does not know how to cook. Neither my mother nor my sisters or I have the necessary training in housework to school them.'

'I have,' said Mrs Kennedy. She turned to her nephew. 'Be so good as to order the carriage immediately.'

'Please, ma'am,' begged Isabella, startled at the speed with which help was being offered and not sure now that she wanted it, 'I am sure we can manage.'

'Poor lamb. I am sure you cannot. Don't come with us, Guy. This is woman's work, and men are sore out o' place in the kitchen.'

And ladies, thought Isabella haughtily, and then chided herself and wondered if she would ever come to terms with being the poor Miss Beverley.

So when the carriage was brought round, she meekly went out with Mrs Kennedy, whose eyes were flashing with an almost religious zeal.

'And what is the name of this cratur who is holding sway in your kitchen?' she asked.

'A Mrs Pearce.'

'Right you are, m'dear. You leave her to me.'

Isabella kept glancing sideways at the bulk of Mrs Kennedy as they were driven to Brookfield House. What a quiz of a bonnet! How her sisters would giggle. Thank goodness her parents were too cast down to be chilly.

By the time they reached home, she was heartily wishing she had never gone to appeal to Mrs Kennedy for help. Barry, who had travelled on the backstrap, helped them from the carriage.

'Some tea or a glass of wine, perhaps?'

'No, no, m'dear,' said Mrs Kennedy, following her into the house. 'Civilities later. Work first. Lead the way to the kitchen.'

Isabella reluctantly led the way through to the back quarters and pushed open the kitchen door. A small boy was washing dishes in the scullery. Mrs Pearce was sitting at the table with a glass of gin and hot.

'What's this?' demanded Mrs Pearce, staggering to her feet.

'I am Mrs Kennedy of Perival and I am here to train you in your job.'

'I don't need no training,' said the cook drunkenly.

Mrs Kennedy put her hands on her hips and stared

41

at the cook. 'You are beyond training. Pack your traps and get out.'

'You have no right . . .' began Mrs Pearce, but Mrs Kennedy's late husband had been an army officer and she had followed him on many a campaign and had adopted his military manner when necessary.

'OUT!' she shouted. 'And be damned to ye for a useless hussy.'

When Mrs Pearce had cursed her way out, Isabella sat wearily down at the kitchen table. 'What do we do now?' she asked.

'Who employed this Pearce cratur?'

'Mr Ducket, Papa's secretary. I saw his horse when we arrived.'

The Beverleys and Mr Ducket felt that Mrs Kennedy had descended on them like a whirlwind. Mrs Kennedy drove off with Mr Ducket into the town, placed a board outside the inn asking for the services of a cook-housekeeper, and then dealt briskly with the applicants and then, to Mr Ducket's consternation, settled on a pensioned army sergeant with one leg who said he could do a deal of plain cooking and would be quick to learn the 'fancy stuff.' His name was Joshua Evans. He had grey hair, a thin, clever face, and an engaging smile.

His bags were collected and he was removed to the kitchen of Brookfield House, where Mrs Kennedy donned a voluminous apron and both got to work.

Mrs Kennedy refused to stay for dinner. She kissed

Isabella on the cheek and said she would return on the morrow to further Joshua's education and have a talk to the maids.

Dinner was simple but excellent. Joshua had told the maids to be as quiet as possible when serving the meal, not to rush, not to get flustered, and they managed very well. The Beverley sisters, with the exception of Isabella, entertained their mother and father with impersonations of Mrs Kennedy until Isabella told them sharply to stop.

'Are we going to malign and sneer at the one person who has helped us?' she cried.

'Oh, we'll talk about something else,' said Jessica. 'Papa, this Mr Judd. What kind of person is he?'

'Nothing much,' said Sir William. 'Lucky at cards. Dedicated gambler. Foxy-looking fellow.'

'And what is Mrs Judd like?' asked Belinda.

Sir William leaned back in his chair. There was a little colour in his cheeks and he was quite sober. The organization of his servants by Mrs Kennedy had enlivened him, as had the good food. 'There is no Mrs Judd,' he said. 'The fellow is a bachelor.'

Six pairs of eyes stared at him. The daughters of Mannerling digested this fascinating piece of information.

'But, Papa,' said Isabella slowly, 'why did you not mention this before?'

'I did not want to talk about the man. He took every-thing from me, but I have to admit, he won fair and square.'

Isabella clasped her hands and looked at him

earnestly. 'Whoever marries Mr Judd will be mistress of Mannerling.'

'Oh, Isabella,' cried Jessica, forgetting her sister's monumental failure in the marriage stakes of London. '*You* could marry him and then we could all go home.'

'Home,' echoed the others. 'Home.'

THREE

Your beautiful bit who hath all eyes upon her;
* That her honesty sells for a hogo of honour;*
Whose lightness and brightness doth cast such a
*   splendour,*
That none are thought fit but the stars to attend her,
Though now she seems pleasant and sweet to the seme,
Will be damnable mouldy a hundred years hence.

THOMAS JORDAN

'You must use Lord Fitzpatrick to practise on,' said Jessica.

The sisters were sitting on the grass outside their home on a fine day. Mrs Kennedy's voice could occasionally be heard sounding from the house as she lectured the maids.

'What makes you think I need practice?' demanded Isabella huffily.

'Because of your failure at the Season,' remarked Lizzie quietly. The rest looked at her nervously. She had finally voiced what they had all been thinking.

'Oh, if I am such a failure,' exclaimed Isabella, 'perhaps one of the rest of you should go after this Mr Judd.'

'It is your duty as the eldest and most beautiful,' said Jessica firmly. 'Besides, I noticed at the ball that you were much at your ease with Lord Fitzpatrick. If you behave with this Mr Judd as you behave with Lord Fitzpatrick, then there should be no trouble at all.'

'What age is this Mr Judd?' asked Lizzie.

'In his thirties,' remarked Abigail. 'Betty, the new maid, is a relative of one of the maids at Mannerling and she told me.'

'But this man is a hardened gamester,' said Lizzie, 'and yet Isabella must sacrifice herself for the sake of getting our old home back.'

'Pooh, as to that, I would marry the devil himself if I could get Mannerling back,' said Isabella. 'But you are right in your strictures. I had been brought up to suppose that our wealth and rank could get us any man I wanted and so I was too stiff and formal. And I do not think it will further any friendship with Viscount Fitzpatrick if we sit here lazily while his aunt does the work that we should be doing.'

'How can we?' asked Abigail. 'We know nothing of housework.'

Isabella rose gracefully to her feet. 'Then it is time we all found out. I think Mrs Kennedy should instruct *us.*'

They looked at her with varying degrees of horror. 'Why not?' demanded Isabella. 'Do we sit here uselessly with the whole day to pass?'

Her sisters followed her reluctantly indoors and explained to Mrs Kennedy that they would be most grateful if she could introduce them to the arts of housewifery. 'To be sure I can,' said the good lady, her round face beaming with pleasure. 'I am just going to the kitchen to school that new cook of yours in some fancier dishes.'

At first the girls stood around sulkily, listening to Mrs Kennedy's lectures on sauces, but when she turned her attention to them and began to instruct them on how to make pastry, they began at first reluctantly to work and then with increasing enthusiasm as pastry was rolled out for tarts. By the time little fruit tarts had been placed tenderly in the oven, they felt they could hardly wait to see the results.

Joshua Evans, the cook, limped about on his wooden leg and smiled at their enthusiasm and then, at Mrs Kennedy's invitation, sat down with them at the kitchen table when the tarts were ready, to sample some of them. Isabella was so proud of her efforts that she ran outside to fetch Barry to join the party.

Lady Beverley opened the door of the kitchen and stood transfixed at the sight of her elegant daughters hob-nobbing with the servants. She then retreated but waited until Mrs Kennedy had left before she summoned the girls to the drawing room and gave them a blistering lecture on the folly of not knowing their place and encouraging familiarity among the servants.

'It is all part of the plan,' said Jessica. 'Isabella is to practise flirting with the viscount so that she may learn how to woo this Mr Judd. Besides, Mama, it was rather fun. And we are to go to Perival tomorrow to learn how to make over gowns.'

'Make over gowns!' Lady Beverley raised her thin white hands in horror. 'Why?'

'Because the ones we have cannot last forever,' said Lizzie.

'But if Isabella is to marry Mr Judd, then we will be back at Mannerling and all will be as it was,' wailed Lady Beverley.

Are we all mad? wondered Isabella suddenly. But she said aloud, 'Even if I were to marry this Mr Judd, I could not possibly say to him, "I am moving my whole family back into residence and I want you to return all our jewellery and I want everything to be as it was." '

There was a sad little silence as they all digested this grim fact. Then Lizzie said, 'Well, in any case, I think we should all go to Perival tomorrow. I enjoy doing things and not sitting idle.'

'How are you to get there?' demanded Lady Beverley.

'Mrs Kennedy is sending a carriage,' said Isabella.

'You mean a *carridge*,' pointed out Jessica and they all, with the exception of Isabella, giggled.

Lady Beverley sighed. 'That one should have to associate with such people.'

'People like Mrs Kennedy have warmth and kindness, so perhaps that is why such as she appears strange to us,' said Isabella wrathfully. She swept from the room and banged the door behind her in a most unladylike way.

'Dear me,' said Lady Beverley, 'I do hope this Mrs Kennedy is not going to be a lowering influence on the manners of our dear Isabella.'

'Perhaps her manners will need to be lowered enough to chase after a gamester,' said Lizzie quietly, but no one paid any attention to her.

Isabella went in search of Barry and found him working in the small vegetable garden at the back of the house. She sat down on an upturned box and surveyed him gravely.

'Where do you come from, Barry?'

He leaned on his hoe. 'Do you mean, miss, what was I doing afore I come here?'

'Yes.'

'Oh, all sorts of things, but I was in the military for ten years, which is why I get along just great with Joshua in the kitchen. I came out three years ago and worked at bits o' this and bits o' that. I was always knacky at repairing things and got enough work to augment my pension. Not much of a drinking or baccy man, nor do I gamble, and so I was comfortable enough. Then Mr Ducket was applying for servants for here and so I got the job. Free lodgings and my pension. I am a lucky man, Miss Isabella.'

'How do you find us?'

'That's not for me to say, miss.'

'Do you not sometimes think of us as peculiarly useless specimens of humanity?'

'Miss Isabella! I have never criticized my betters and don't intend to start now. A Tory, me, and proud o' it. Who's been putting Whig notions into your pretty head, miss?'

'No one. Straitened circumstances are making me

look at the world a new way. It is as if Mannerling cast a spell on all of us.'

'It did that,' he said quietly. 'If I may be so bold as to speak plain, miss, Brookfield may seem a come-down in the world, but it's a solid house and can be made comfortable. You will forget Mannerling in time.'

Isabella shook her head. How could such as Barry understand that every part of Mannerling, every stick and stone seemed part of her?

The following day, when she was seated with her sisters in the drawing room at Perival, Isabella wondered whether this journey might prove to be a failure. She was anxious to begin her 'lessons,' namely, learning to flirt, rather than dressmaking. But soon she became as absorbed as the others in learning how to place neat stitches, in how a few new coloured ribbons could decorate and change the appearance of an old gown. Most ladies when they felt their gowns were out of fashion, or had been seen too much, sold them, but the Beverleys had given them to the poor, who should have therefore been the most elegantly attired paupers in England, but they had sold the clothes for much-needed money and kept their rags. How profligate she and her sisters had been, thought Isabella as she stitched away. She remembered several pretty gowns which she had given away after they had been worn only a few times. Her mind worked away busily over the problem of the new owner of Mannerling. Was he in residence? She should have asked the maid, Betty. But surely Mrs Kennedy would know.

'Is Mr Judd at Mannerling?' she asked.

'I believe so,' replied Mrs Kennedy. 'He arrived yesterday. There is a great fuss among the servants. He said he did not need so many, and of course, being a single man, he has no need of all those lady's-maids. Goodness knows where the females will find employment in the country! You will probably find several of your old servants on your doorstep looking for employ.'

'Oh, really!' Jessica sniffed. 'Too late. They were not loyal to us, so why should we be loyal to them?'

'Fortunately our changed circumstances have made the decision for us,' said Lizzie quietly. 'We cannot afford any more servants.'

Jessica looked at her impatiently and then realized to her horror that she had almost been on the point of blurting out that when Isabella was mistress of Mannerling, she could employ as many servants as she wanted.

'Has anyone seen Mr Judd?' Isabella was asking.

'There, now,' said Mrs Kennedy, waxing the end of a thread, 'I do believe the Stoppards called the minute Mr Judd was in residence.'

'The Stoppards have not called on us,' said Isabella, thinking again that surely the vicar might have at least paid a visit to ask how they went on.

'He's a poor sort of cratur, that vicar, and so I am thinking,' said Mrs Kennedy. 'And I don't trust that Mary Stoppard either. Watching, always watching with those black eyes of hers while compliments, as false as anything, pour from her lips.'

51

Isabella felt uncomfortable. She had always taken the Stoppards's oily blandishments as the Beverleys's due. It looked as if no one at all had really cared for them.

It was at that moment that the viscount walked into the room. He stood for a moment in the doorway, his expression serious as he noticed the distress on Isabella's face.

'Why, 'tis Guy, come to join the ladies,' cried Mrs Kennedy.

'I wondered if Miss Isabella would care to take a turn in the gardens with me.'

'Gladly.' Isabella rose, pleased that she was wearing one of her prettiest morning gowns of white muslin with an overdress of white lace. She would have been amazed had she been able to read Mrs Kennedy's thoughts. Mrs Kennedy privately thought Isabella looked sadly overdressed. All her gowns were obviously expensive but lacked the style they should have had considering what the Beverleys had probably paid for them.

In the gardens, the viscount drew Isabella's arm through his own and glanced down at her in amusement. 'I feel I should be leading you down the aisle.'

Isabella looked up at him in alarm. Was this a proposal of marriage?'

'Your gown,' he said gently. 'All that white lace.'

'Oh!' Isabella blushed in confusion. 'It does not please you, my lord?'

'You please me, but you could enhance your looks further with something less . . . fussy.'

'And you the arbiter of high fashion!'

'Not I. My aunt, however, has a keen eye.'

'Mrs Kennedy!'

'She was once a dasher but now dresses for comfort.'

'And she has been criticizing my gowns to you?'

'She has a maternal concern for you, that is all. You and your sisters have provided her with a new lease of life. She does not mean to interfere or criticize. All her actions are prompted by kindness and concern.'

'I agree about the kindness and concern. But you should leave any strictures on fashion to your aunt instead of repeating them to me. What if I were to say to you that my father disapproved of the cut of your coat?'

'My coat is an excellent cut and I would disagree with him. Now if you were to tell me that Sir William disapproved of my Irishness, that I would believe.'

'You must consider us too high in the instep.'

'A trifle.'

'And I must take you to task, my lord. When you called on us at Mannerling during our last week and I did not wish to see you, it was because I was angry with you.'

'Oh, my poor heart! What had I done?'

'I feel you knew of my father's gambling and that we were shortly to be ruined and were hinting such. Why did you not come out and speak to me direct about it? Perhaps we could have stopped him before he lost all.'

'I had only heard rumours that he was playing deep at the tables of St James's. And I have seen many men lose all they had. But I did not know for certain. It seemed an impertinence to tell you about your father without actual knowledge.'

Isabella practised a flirtatious look at him. 'You are forgiven.'

Then she wondered if her look had been too bold because it was answered with a quizzical look of his own.

'You have not looked at the gardens,' he chided.

They were in a walled garden now. Peach trees were espaliered against the walls. The neat beds were full of herbs and vegetables. Isabella bent down and plucked a sprig of lavender from a bordering hedge. 'The smell of the herbs is delicious.'

'Most of the gardening here might depress you. At the moment we are concentrating on vegetables rather than flowers, but even here we have things like lavender. No grand vistas or temples, Miss Isabella.'

She gave a little sigh. 'I took so very much for granted. I thought life would go on, undemanding and pleasant, like a well-oiled machine.'

'But you had a Season in London, and a Season usually means a husband, particularly for someone as beautiful as you are and as rich as you were until recently. That would have meant change.'

Isabella gave him a puzzled look.

He laughed. 'I swear you did not even consider the prospect of change a husband would bring. Was he a shadowy figure in your mind who would come and live somewhere in Mannerling and not disturb the even tenor of your days?'

This was exactly what Isabella had thought.

'Did you not think a husband might even mean love, passion, and children to follow?' he asked.

Isabella coloured up angrily. 'Shall we talk of something else?'

'As you will.' He led her out of the walled garden. 'Now here,' he went on, waving a hand towards the shaggy lawns, 'there is much to be done. As you can see, very few flowers or trees, and I am anxious to see some trees while I am still alive. To that end I have ordered some pretty ones to be transported fully grown and planted here next week. Then I think an ornamental lake over there.'

Isabella recollected that she was supposed to be learning to flirt, but she grew interested in his plans for the gardens and made several suggestions which were so warmly accepted that her enthusiasm grew. He then proposed they should return to join the others for tea and he would show her the plans he had drawn up.

Jessica watched carefully as Isabella and the viscount stood at a desk in the corner of the drawing room, poring over plans. Isabella was not flirting, but in her dealings with the viscount there was an easy friendliness. Jessica thought Isabella must be a very good actress indeed, not realizing that her sister found the viscount pleasant company and in her enthusiasm over his plans for his gardens had forgotten his uncomfortable remarks about marriage and about her dress, although she did remember the latter when she finally joined her sisters for tea.

'I believe,' she said to Mrs Kennedy, 'that you find my style of dress a trifle fussy.'

Mrs Kennedy looked furiously at her nephew. 'And aren't we the blabbermouth now,' she said wrathfully. She turned contritely to Isabella. 'Faith, my chuck, all I did remark, and it was not meant for your pretty ears, was that your grand London dressmaker used the finest materials but had a poor eye for line.'

Jessica's cynical eye raked Mrs Kennedy's squat figure and old-fashioned gown. 'You're looking at me, Miss Jessica,' said Mrs Kennedy, 'as if wondering what an old body like me can know of style. But I dress now in me old age for comfort. I can still turn out a good line if I put me mind to it. I can see you don't believe me. Well, I tell you, when you send back the carridge, send that gown back along with it and you'll never believe the difference.'

Isabella calmly agreed. Everything must be done to keep close to Perival, where she could practise on this viscount.

On the road home, the sisters decided to call at the vicarage to see what news of the new tenant could be gleaned from Mary, but they learned from the vicarage servant that Mr and Miss Stoppard were both at Mannerling.

'Creeping toads,' commented Jessica as they drove off. 'Do you realize, Isabella, that we are going to have to force Papa to go and see this Mr Judd, else we shall perhaps never get an invitation to Mannerling?'

'I do not think he will be able to even bear to think of that idea,' said Isabella.

But she was proved wrong. Sir William had learned little from his financial disaster and still had the gambler's superstitious mind. He had seen two magpies that morning and that surely meant Isabella would marry Mr Judd and reclaim Mannerling, and so Barry was sent to Hedgefield to rent a carriage and Sir William set out the next day.

On his return he said bleakly that they were all expected for tea the next day and then took himself off to his study, emerging to join them for dinner and show them all that he was quite drunk again.

Mrs Kennedy had sent a footman over to collect Isabella's gown and also a note to say she had caught a summer cold and would not be visiting them for a few days. Isabella was relieved. She did not want Mrs Kennedy around when they prepared to set off for Mannerling in case that lady overheard anything and guessed their plans.

Another rented carriage. Isabella for the first time began to wonder just how much money was left, if any. She privately thought this Mr Judd should have been thoughtful enough to send a carriage for them.

Perhaps she was the only unhappy member of the party as they all set out, although Lizzie was very quiet. The others were elated, confident that Isabella would win the prize.

But they all fell silent as the carriage rolled up the long drive of Mannerling. The butler met them at the door, his face wooden and unsmiling, just as if he had never worked for them. He led the way upstairs to the Green Saloon and Isabella began to feel increasingly nervous.

But Mannerling was crying to her to come home. The elegant staircase, the painted ceilings, the cool rooms – all belonged to the Beverleys, not to this interloper.

She stiffened her spine and followed her parents into the Green Saloon.

She received two shocks. The first was the appearance of Mr Judd. She had been imagining a man somewhat like the viscount, but this Mr Judd was tall and thin with sandy hair, light-green eyes, and a foxy face. The second shock was the presence of the Stoppards, Mary in particular, both looking very much at home, and Mary was acting as hostess, directing the servants as to where to lay the tea-things, and making the tea herself.

Isabella's eyes ranged round the room. Some of their beautiful and elegant furniture had been replaced by nasty Jacobean stuff, heavily carved and sombre. She quickly averted her eyes and met those of Mary Stoppard, black, unfathomable.

'Well, now,' said Mr Judd when they were all seated, 'this is indeed a bevy of beauties.'

Isabella pretended he was the viscount and gave him a warm smile. 'You will turn our heads, sir.'

'And you, Miss Isabella, must turn the heads of all who set eyes on you,' replied Mr Judd, and gave a high cackle of laughter.

'We all expect our Miss Isabella to be snatched up by some lucky gentleman soon,' said Mary. 'Of course, after last Season . . .' Her voice trailed away. She signalled to a footman. 'John, take the caraway cake to Lady Beverley. Lady Beverley was always fond of Mannerling caraway cake.'

And so, having effectively reminded Isabella of her failure to secure a husband at the Season and Lady Beverley of her changed circumstances, Mary smiled benignly all round.

'Thank you for those books you lent me, Mr Judd,' said the vicar. 'Very interesting.' He was a small, round, plump man with a white face and those black eyes his daughter had inherited from him.

'What books?' asked Isabella before she could stop herself. 'Bailey's *Guide to the Tuif*?'

Her sisters gave her reproachful looks. 'Not at all,' said the vicar. 'You do Mr Judd an injustice.'

'An injustice,' echoed Mary faintly.

'I was joking,' said Isabella. 'I am anxious to see any changes you have made to Mannerling, Mr Judd.'

'Come,' said that gentleman, 'I will be delighted to show you.' He led Isabella from the room. The sisters exchanged covert, triumphant little glances.

In the Long Gallery, she gave an exclamation of dismay. 'Where are the Beverley ancestors, Mr Judd?'

'Got fine pictures of my own, Miss Isabella, and they ain't my ancestors, after all. Put them in the attics.'

Isabella looked up at the 'fine' pictures, which were mostly of horses: horses racing, horses hunting, horses just standing staring straight ahead. She wanted to say to him that if he did not want the Beverley ancestors, why did he not give them to Sir William, but pride kept her quiet. 'What very fine animals,' she said instead.

'Prime bits of blood, Miss Isabella. Come, I have

more in the Blue Saloon.' And so he had, paintings of dogs and slaughtered game being added to paintings of more horses. The pretty landscapes, seascapes, and rural scenes had all gone.

'Where are the pictures that were here?' asked Isabella. 'In the attics as well?'

'No, I sent those up to London for sale.'

Isabella bit back an exclamation of dismay. But she must charm this man. Mannerling must belong to them again. She fanned herself and said, 'Mannerling is indeed fortunate to have a new owner of such taste and distinction.'

'You think so? Coming from a beauty like yourself, Miss Isabella, I am flattered. You would be an ornament to any great house.'

She forced herself to give him an intimate smile and then lowered those long eyelashes of hers. He seized her hand and raised it to his lips. 'Oh, Mr Judd,' said Isabella, copying the fluttering manner of the debutantes of London, to whom she had only so recently considered herself infinitely superior.

'Tell you what,' said Mr Judd, who appeared highly pleased with her, 'come over next Tuesday on your own and I'll give you a tour of the grounds. Plan some improvements there.'

'I am most honoured. May I beg you to send a carriage for me?'

He laughed as if the idea of the Beverleys being carriageless amused him. 'I'll come and get you myself.' He squeezed her hand again and then led her back to the Green Saloon.

'Now not a word of this to Mrs Kennedy,' cautioned Isabella on the road home after she had regaled them with a description of Mr Judd's advances.

'And what is anything we may say or do or plan to do the concern of that burly-burly Irishwoman?' demanded Lady Beverley. There was colour in her cheeks for the first time since disaster had struck them.

Isabella had an impulse to cry out that such as Mrs Kennedy were above vulgar machinations. Instead she said, 'If I am to practise on Lord Fitzpatrick; he would not be so available, nor his aunt, were they to know of my pursuit of Mr Judd. Besides, they are the only friends we have. No one else in the county has shown any compassion for our plight.'

'I hate that Mary Stoppard,' said Jessica. 'How she used to creep around us! Now she is acting as if she were the mistress of Mannerling. You do not think Mr Judd will marry *her*?'

But the others laughed at the very idea of any man preferring a dumpy vicar's daughter to the beauty of the county.

Isabella sent Barry over to Perival the next day with a letter to Mrs Kennedy in which she said she hoped that lady's cold was improving. Barry returned with a letter from the viscount. He wrote that he would ride over later that day and bring Satan with him in the hope that she might find time to go for a ride with him.

Finding to her surprise that she was really looking forward to seeing him again, and that it was as good a way as any to pass the time until she should see

Mannerling again, Isabella was in high good humour by the time he arrived.

The viscount privately thought that the removal to Brookfield House had improved the Beverleys. There was an easygoing family atmosphere in the square house, and Sir William was looking much improved and seemed to have become reconciled to his new life.

Isabella and the viscount rode out along the road and then turned off down a bridle-path. The viscount was content to let his horse amble as he talked. He said his aunt's coughs and sneezes could be heard all over Perival. He said he was looking forward to the transformation of the gardens.

'Mr Judd is to take me on a tour of improvements he has made to the gardens at Mannerling,' said Isabella, forgetting her good resolutions in his easy company.

He reined in his horses and she did the same. 'You have met him?'

'Yes, myself and the family went there yesterday for tea.'

'That must have been very distressing for you.'

'Why?'

'I saw Judd at the tables in London. Now, I would describe him as weak and devious and thoroughly nasty.'

But Isabella did not want to listen to any criticism of her future husband, for, most of the time now, she was back at Mannerling, the pictures of the ancestors hung once more in the Long Gallery, and she and her sisters, calm, rich, and elegant, strolling in the grounds.

'I found him interesting and good company,' she said.

His blue eyes, which a moment before had been merry, were now filled with contempt. 'Oho, I see your plan. You would marry this creature. You would throw away any chance of life and love for a pile of bricks and glass. You weary me suddenly, Miss Isabella.'

'I never said anything about marriage!' Isabella's face flamed.

'Any family with any dignity and self-respect would keep away from a shallow gamester who robbed them of lands, home, and inheritance. I hope for your sake that the idiot burns Mannerling to the ground and sets you all free!'

He spurred his horse and rode away through the trees down the bridle-path. Isabella urged her mount after him. This was all wrong. How could she practise flirting with one man if she had made her preference for another so plain? When she eventually caught up with him he had reined in again at the edge of the woods and was staring out across the countryside.

'My lord,' said Isabella, 'you must not think that just because we paid a visit to Mannerling that we have any deep plot in mind. Do realize that my old home meant a great deal to me. Come, let us be friends again.'

He turned and studied her. Her beautiful face looked pleadingly up into his. A light breeze blew an errant brown curl against her cheek. His face softened. 'I have seen houses take over people before, Miss Isabella. I have also seen men accept their losses stoically at the tables and then go away and blow their brains out.'

'My father . . .' she began in alarm.

Lord Fitzpatrick privately thought that Sir William was too selfish to ever dream of taking his own life.

'I do not think your father will do himself any harm whatsoever,' he said.

'I just hope he never gambles again.' Isabella was anxious now to turn the conversation away from Mr Judd and Mannerling.

The viscount wanted to point out cynically that he had never yet met a reformed gambler. Was Sir William now gambling in his mind on the hope that this eldest daughter would get his home back for him? But Isabella and Judd! It could not be possible. She was too young, too fresh, too beautiful to ever contemplate an alliance with such a man.

But the viscount, who was thirty, had forgotten the difference between his age and that of such as nineteen-year-old Isabella. He did not know that Isabella had never thought of love, that she was unawakened and innocent and thought, if she thought at all, of marriage as a sort of business partnership and had not the slightest idea of how one conceived children.

And so he was quickly restored to good humour. He told her a story of how one of his Irish servants had been found shaking all over and the other servants had diagnosed whirligigitis and had pushed him in the pond, water being supposed to be the best cure, and how Mrs Kennedy had practically had to rescue the poor man from drowning for he could not swim, and had offered the correct diagnosis: that he was shaking all over because he had drunk a considerable amount of the viscount's brandy in the servants' hall the night before.

They rode on amicably. 'What a wonderful summer,' sighed Isabella.

He looked at the sky. 'Not for long, I think,' he remarked. 'The wind has changed.'

'Oh, dear,' she said, thinking that her promised tour of the Mannerling gardens was only two days away.

'But the countryside needs rain,' he said, wondering at her obvious anxiety.

She gave a little shrug, suddenly hoping he would not call on her on Tuesday and find she had gone to Mannerling.

FOUR

So long as all the increased wealth which modern progress brings goes but to build up great fortunes, to increase luxury and make sharper the contrast between the House of Have and the House of Want, progress is not real and cannot be permanent.

HENRY GEORGE

Isabella set out for Mannerling on the Tuesday, and her mother, father, and sisters stood outside Brookfield House to wave her goodbye as if she were going off to the wars.

She was sharply aware that the coachman on the box and the footmen on the backstrap had once worked for the Beverleys and might remark on this odd send-off.

She found herself anxiously awaiting the first sight of Mannerling, knowing somehow that the magic spell her old home cast on her would stiffen her resolve, because without it, a nasty little voice of common sense was telling her that she was pursuing a gentleman in whom she had no interest whatsoever except as a means of returning to her beloved home.

Betty, the small maid, elevated to lady's-maid for the occasion and wearing one of Lizzie's old gowns, sat looking as solemn as a well-behaved child. Isabella was wearing one of her more dashing hats, a straw embellished with silk roses of different colours around the crown. She was dressed in a light muslin gown in shades of delicate lilac, darkening towards the hem to near purple. The sun no longer shone, a bad omen, and a blustery wind from the west rustled the parched leaves of the trees on either side of the road.

It was when the carriage was turning in at the gates of Mannerling that she began to wonder whether this visit were not too unconventional. Mr Judd had no lady in residence, and although she, Isabella, had a maid with her, it was surely not correct to visit a single man in his home.

Therefore she experienced a surge of gladness and relief to be initially received in the drawing room by Mrs Judd, Mr Judd's mother, a tall, thin widow with a perpetual air of disapproval.

After the introductions and pleasantries were over, Mrs Judd said, 'This was your home, was it not?'

'Yes, ma'am,' said Isabella, stealing a look around and noticing several very pretty ornaments which had decorated the mantelpiece were no longer there.

Mrs Judd was dressed in black, as befitted her widowed status, shiny black decorated with jet, which gave her a reptilian look. She folded lace-mittened hands in her lap and commented, 'I have told Ajax time and again that gamblers always ruin themselves sooner or later.'

At first Isabella was too surprised to learn that Mr Judd was called Ajax to take offence, but then the full import of Mrs Judd's words sank into her brain. She rose and said with quiet dignity to Mr Judd, 'I am anxious to see the gardens, sir, and perhaps we should begin now because it looks like rain.'

'Gladly,' he said with that foxy smile of his. When they were outside, he pointed his stick in the direction of a stand of trees. 'I'm getting those cut down for a start,' he said. 'Block the view.'

'Oh, no, Mr Judd,' said Isabella, shaken. 'Capability Brown himself designed those vistas. Do you not see how those trees are part of the harmonious plan?'

'Well, well, *I* don't like 'em and it's my place now. Hey, now, though, if it troubles you so much, I'll leave the trees for the moment. But you'll like what I've got planned round the back. Come.'

A damp breeze blew against Isabella's cheek. The rain could not be far off. They walked around the side of the house to the back. 'Now, see that temple thing over there,' he commanded.

The Greek temple stood on a mound overlooking the ornamental lake, its slender columns whiter than ever against the darkening sky.

'Oh, yes,' sighed Isabella, thinking of how on sunny days she and her sisters would get the servants to carry a picnic hamper to the temple. Then they would take a boat out on the lake. She closed her eyes for a second, remembering happy, peaceful, innocent days gone forever.

'Going to knock it down,' said Mr Judd with satisfaction.

'Why?' asked Isabella faintly.

'Having a ruin is all the crack, one of those Gothic things, all moss, and with a hermit. Have that instead. Got to have a hermit.'

'And do you know a hermit?'

'Don't need to be a real one. One of the servants will do it. That footman, John, now he's a trifle too uppity for my taste. If he wants to continue to collect his wages, he can be a hermit and put on some rags instead of that plush uniform.'

Raindrops rattled down on Isabella's bonnet. 'We must return to shelter,' he said. 'Poxy rain.'

Isabella felt like crying. If he was prepared to smash down the beautiful temple, what other horrors had he in store for Mannerling?

When they were back in the drawing room, Mrs Judd presiding over the teacups, Mr Judd said, 'I'm thinking of giving a ball here, get to know the neighbours. Is that secretary still about?'

'Until the end of the week,' said Isabella.

'Better get him to furnish me with a list.'

'Ajax,' reprimanded his mother, 'you cannot be contemplating a ball when your poor father is scarcely cold in his grave!'

'Pooh, died over a year ago.'

Mrs Judd took out a starched handkerchief and applied it to her eyes.

'How did your father die?' asked Isabella.

'Blew his brains out,' said Mr Judd succinctly.

'I wish that nice Miss Stoppard was here,' moaned Mrs Judd. '*She* is all sentiment.'

'I am deeply sorry to learn of your loss,' said Isabella. 'My husband would never have let us live here,' wailed Mrs Judd. 'The place is too big.'

'He could never have afforded to live here,' remarked her son with heartless satisfaction. He was standing by the fireplace and ran his hand lovingly over the marble mantel in the way one caresses a favourite pet.

Isabella stole a covert look around the room again. Drawing rooms, because of the custom – still regarded on the Contintent as a form of English barbarity – of separating the men and the women at the end of a meal, had come to be regarded as the preserve of the ladies, and this was usually reflected in the lighter furniture, knick-knacks, portfolios of water-colours, work-tables, and the latest ladies' magazines. But the console table at Mannerling now only held sporting magazines, a gamebag lay discarded just inside the door, and a fishing-rod was propped against the window shutters.

'I am feeling poorly,' complained Mrs Judd. 'Be so good as to excuse me, Miss Isabella.'

And so convention demanded that Isabella took her leave. Mr Judd walked her downstairs and out to the carriage. They stood for a moment under an umbrella held over them by a footman.

'Tell you what,' said Mr Judd, 'I'll take you for a drive next week. Tuesday again, hey?'

Isabella dimpled and curtsied. 'I consider myself honoured, sir.'

'Call for you at two.'

And so, as Isabella was driven off, she fought down that constantly monitoring voice which was telling her that he ought to have asked her parents' permission first. The farther she was driven from Mannerling, the more awful Mr Judd and his mother seemed. But surely no sacrifice was too great to regain Mannerling.

When she arrived home, she was hustled into a little parlour on the ground floor by her sisters, anxious to hear her news.

They gave exclamations of dismay when she told them about the trees and the temple.

But Jessica said stoutly, 'All that can be restored when you are married, Isabella.'

'I wish I were a gambler,' sighed Isabella. 'Then I would play him at cards for Mannerling.'

Lizzie looked at Isabella, her green eyes shining. 'You cannot, but Lord Fitzpatrick could . . . if you asked him.'

Isabella shook her head. 'My lord thinks that the best thing that could happen to the Beverleys is that Mr Judd should set fire to the place and burn it down!'

'What a monster!' cried Abigail. 'But does Mr Judd appear at all *warm* towards you, Isabella?'

'Ye-es, yes, he does. He is to take me driving next week.' The door opened and Sir William and Lady Beverley entered.

'How went it?' asked Sir William eagerly.

'I met Mrs Judd,' said Isabella.

'Angels preserve me!' Lady Beverley put a fluttering hand to her bosom. 'He is married!'

'No, Mama, his mother.'

'Ah, the relief! And how did you find the lady? Is she elegant? How was she gowned?'

'Mrs Judd is a widow,' said Isabella cautiously, 'and still grieves for the loss of her husband.'

'When did he die?'

'A year ago, I gather. He blew his brains out.'

'Merciful heavens. Why?'

'I do not know,' retorted Isabella sharply. 'Perhaps gambling runs in the family. Mr Judd is to take me driving next Tuesday.'

Sir William rubbed his hands. 'It's as good as in the bag.'

'What is, Papa?'

'Your marriage to him, of course.'

'Tell Papa about the temple,' urged Lizzie.

'Mr Judd intends to knock down the temple and replace it with a ruin. He is going to put footman John in it to act the part of a hermit.'

Sir William walked to the window and stared out at the rain. Raindrops gathered on the window and ran down it like tears. 'Well, well,' he said in a stifled voice, 'such things can be put back again.'

'How?' asked Lizzie, her pointed chin on her hands. 'After the wedding, does Isabella say, "I want that temple back"? And he says, "Yes, dear"?'

'Gentlemen can be coaxed,' said Jessica loftily. 'If he loves Isabella, he will do anything for her.'

Love, thought Isabella, what is love? She did not read romances. 'Do you not think, Mama,' she ventured, 'that it is extremely odd in Mr Judd to make arrangements to take me for a drive without asking the permission of my parents first?'

'It shows that Mr Judd feels on easy terms with us,' protested Lady Beverley.

'He is to give a ball,' said Isabella.

'He will never give one in such style as we did,' said Sir William over his shoulder.

Isabella half-closed her eyes, remembering in dismay how much had been squandered on that last ball, from the new bed hangings to the gold swords for the footmen.

Barry came in with a basket of logs and kindling.

'Begging your pardon,' he said, 'but the day has turned damp and cold. I thought you might like a fire.'

Lady Beverley nodded. Barry set the fire and lit it and soon there was a cheerful crackling of burning wood.

He retreated with the empty log basket over his arm.

'Excuse me,' said Isabella hurriedly. She followed Barry through to the kitchen. 'Where is Joshua?' she asked.

'Gone to the market in Hedgefield this morning and not back yet,' said Barry. 'But he will be. He waits until the end and then buys produce cheaply.'

'Oh, dear.' Isabella sat down at the kitchen table. 'I suppose he has a very small amount to spend.'

'Yes, miss, but the gamekeeper at Perival sent over some rabbits and a fine hare and a brace of rooks. Rook pie for dinner tonight.'

'How very kind,' said Isabella.

'I was about to have a jug of ale, Miss Isabella. Would you care for some?'

Isabella nodded. She had never drunk ale. She wondered what she was doing to be so familiar with this servant, but Barry seemed a solid, stable figure in an uncertain world.

He drew a small tankard of ale for her and a larger one for himself.

Isabella waved a hand. 'You may sit down.'

Barry sat down opposite her. He had heard many tales of the incredible pride and haughtiness of the Beverleys, and yet here was the eldest daughter joining him for a tankard of ale.

'May I be so bold as to ask how your visit to Mannerling went, miss?' he asked.

'It was . . . disturbing.' Isabella sighed. It was warm and comfortable in the kitchen. The rain pattered steadily against the windows and dropped down the chimney and hissed on the fire. 'Mr Judd wants to take down a Greek temple and replace it with a ruin. You know, Barry, not a real ruin but one of those fashionable ruins.'

'I have never heard of such a thing, miss!'

'They were all the crack, but the fashion has lately been exploded except in the minds of such as Mr Judd. A gentleman would invite his guests to "come and see the ruin of my ruin." If he already had a ruined something or other, he would embellish it with moss, creepers, and a hermit.'

'The ways of the Quality do be strange, miss.'

'Mrs Judd is in residence.'

'That would be the widow, miss.'

'You appear better informed than I was, Barry.'

'Servants' gossip, miss.'

'And the late Mr Judd shot himself?'

'Yes, miss, lost a fortune at cards.'

'Oh, dear, perhaps it is as well that the son appears to be a luckier gambler.'

'There was a scandal about him. I do hear, miss, that he was once accused of using marked cards.'

'Oh, I am sure that is wrong, Barry. Envious people do say the most dreadful things.'

'Yes, miss. As you say, miss.' Barry buried his nose in his tankard.

'On the other hand, Mr Judd is to take me driving next Tuesday, so I shall be better able to judge his character for myself,' said Isabella. 'I mean, it is always better to make up one's own mind, do you not think so?'

'Yes, miss. Mr Ducket did say as how several of your old servants had called on him, including that lady's-maid of yours, miss, looking for employ.'

Isabella's face hardened. She remembered the gloating look on Maria's face. And yet, and yet, when had any of the Beverleys treated their servants in any way to command loyalty? Sir William did not expect the servants, such as they were at Brookfield House, to turn their faces to the wall when he passed, but that might be because he now regarded Brookfield House as an unwelcome interruption in his life and expected to return to Mannerling. How they were all relying on her! Isabella gave herself a mental shake. Mr

Judd had bad taste, but he seemed amiable and inoffensive enough. She would be able to manage him. Mannerling was so big, she naively thought, that after they were married she need not see very much of him. She would have her own suite of apartments in the west wing.

'We cannot afford any more servants,' she said aloud. 'What will they all do?'

'I s'pose they will go to London,' said Barry. 'They have references, do they not?'

'I believe Mr Ducket saw to all that,' said Isabella. 'Here comes Joshua now. I will leave you.'

She returned to the parlour. Lady Beverley said, 'A footman is arrived from Perival with a request from Mrs Kennedy that you join them for dinner, Isabella. I do not think you should go. If you are to encourage the attentions of Mr Judd, familiarity with such persons is not to be encouraged.'

'Mrs Kennedy and Lord Fitzpatrick are kindness itself,' said Isabella hotly. 'I wish to go, Mama.'

'I forbid it!'

'Then I confess the idea of driving out with Mr Judd next Tuesday wearies me.'

'But you must!'

'Then I have no intention of turning down an invitation to Perival.'

'Oh, go, go,' said Lady Beverley pettishly. 'You will no doubt have a better dinner than we will enjoy here.'

'There is rook pie for dinner.'

'*Rook pie!*' exclaimed Lady Beverley in accents of loathing. 'Since when did the Beverleys eat rook pie?'

'Since they lost all their money,' said Isabella and left the room before her mother could reply.

Isabella was disappointed to learn that the viscount had gone out earlier and had not returned but was expected in time for dinner in half an hour's time. 'So that means,' said Mrs Kennedy, who appeared to have recovered from her cold, 'that we can fit on your gown. I have it here. Take off your dress, Miss Isabella.'

'Here? What if one of your servants should come in?'

'They won't unless I call 'em.'

Isabella slipped off her silk gown and stood in a thin shift and gartered stockings.

'No corset, I see,' said Mrs Kennedy, taking Isabella's altered gown out of a swathing of tissue-paper. 'Now just let me help you into this and tie the tapes, so. There! Go to the looking-glass. Stand on that chair and you will get a full-length view.'

Isabella climbed up on a hard-backed chair and studied her reflection in the glass over the fireplace. The gown had lost its lace overdress and now boasted a low square neckline. Lace now ornamented three deep flounces at the hem. But the altered line was elegant and simple.

'I am so pleased with it,' she said honestly. 'We must beg more classes in needlework from you.'

'Gladly. I have little else to do. Take off that gown and I will pack it for you.'

Isabella slipped off the gown, thinking as she did so that none of the Beverleys until their fall would have dreamt of packing up a gown herself. The door opened and the viscount stood on the threshold. He had a brief glimpse of Isabella, standing in shift and flesh-coloured stockings and pink garters ornamented with rosebuds, before he hurriedly retreated.

'Sure, now, it's sorry I am!' exclaimed a contrite Mrs Kennedy.

'Why?' asked Isabella, who had had her back to the door and had not seen it open.

'I suddenly felt sorry for your plight,' said Mrs Kennedy quickly.

Isabella turned about so that Mrs Kennedy could refasten the tapes of her silk gown. 'Do not worry about me, ma'am,' she said over her shoulder. 'I am become accustomed to it.'

When the viscount finally re-entered, after sending a maid in first to make sure Isabella was respectable, Mrs Kennedy flashed him a warning look to convey to him that Isabella was unaware he had seen her in her undress.

He correctly interpreted the look but wondered if he would ever forget that beautiful sight.

Dinner was a pleasant affair. The viscount encouraged his aunt to tell stories of how she had fared in the wars when she used to accompany her husband. Isabella listened, fascinated. It was all another world, a world of adventure and courage and bravery. Somehow, as Mrs Kennedy talked, the long, easy days of luxury at Mannerling seemed shabby in contrast. And yet, here she was contemplating marriage to Mr Judd so that she could recapture those days.

She found the viscount pleasant to look at with his black hair, bright-blue eyes, and lightly tanned face, but in the same way as she enjoyed looking at a good portrait.

They played Pope Joan after dinner, and then Isabella, looking at the clock, said in dismay that it was past midnight and she would be expected home.

The yawning maid, Betty, was collected and wearily followed her mistress into the carriage, wondering whether the late hours required of a lady's-maid were worth the honour of the position.

'And how did you go, Betty?' Isabella asked after she had made her goodbyes and they were on the road home.

'Very well, ma'am. Because of my supposed position, I dined with the butler and housekeeper in the house-keeper's parlour. Mr O'Brien, the butler, and Mrs Donnell, the housekeeper, are both Irish and rather free and easy in their ways. And yet they have great affection for the master.'

'Did he bring them from some crumbling ruin in Ireland?'

'No, miss, they did say as how Lord Fitzpatrick had a prime bit of property in Kilkenny.'

'Then why did he move to England?'

'He wanted more land, miss. He still has the house and estate in Kilkenny. The Fitzpatricks are a very old family, I believe.'

'I wonder where Mr Judd's family came from.'

'Mr Judd is of the Somerset Judds, an old county family with a bad reputation.'

'Indeed, Betty, I am sure that cannot be true.'

' 'Tis said Mr Judd do come from a long line of wasters and gamblers, miss.'

'That's enough, Betty. I do not listen to servants' gossip.'

'Beg pardon, miss,' said Betty meekly and refrained from pointing out that Isabella had been asking all the questions.

To Isabella's surprise, Mrs Kennedy arrived unheralded the following day and said she was once more ready to give the girls their sewing lessons.

The day seemed to pass quickly for all of them as they practised stitches and pored over fashion magazines, and when Mrs Kennedy said she would send a carriage for them the next day so that they could spread out and study patterns at Perival, where there was more floor space, they all agreed.

Lady Beverley was upset that evening to learn about the proposed visit. 'You should have asked my permission, as should Mrs Kennedy,' she said sternly. 'Too much socializing with the Irish is bound to be disastrous. Lizzie is already punctuating every sentence with "faith" and "sure." '

'Mama,' said Isabella, 'we have received much from Perival in the way of kindness, and presents of game for our larder. Mrs Kennedy is kind and helpful, and why should we not learn the arts of housewifery?'

'Because if you play your cards aright, such labour will not be necessary,' said Lady Beverley.

'I am surprised that *you*, Mama, should even

mention cards!' Lady Beverley folded her pale lips into a disapproving line but did not protest about the visit further.

Isabella found to her surprise that she was disappointed not to see the viscount the following day, nor did Mrs Kennedy say where he was. But they made a merry sewing party, and when Mrs Kennedy invited them all to stay for dinner, they gladly agreed. Somehow Mrs Kennedy created an atmosphere of home such as they had never known, of cosy security and relaxation. The younger ones enjoyed it most. Isabella had always the thought in her mind that somehow she must get Mr Judd to marry her, and Jessica was still plagued by the rigid pride of the Beverleys.

It continued to be rainy and rather cold, and as Tuesday approached, Isabella fought down a wish that it would continue to rain, for Mr Judd could hardly take her driving in a closed carriage, unless he brought his mother along.

But Tuesday dawned bright and fair. None of the sisters had told Mrs Kennedy about Isabella's proposed outing with Mr Judd. The plot was a secret among the Beverleys, and they all had an instinctive feeling that the straightforward and honest Mrs Kennedy would not approve.

Isabella put on the white muslin gown altered by Mrs Kennedy and over it a pelisse of lilac silk. Her bonnet was of white straw, fine and light, and her parasol of lilac silk.

'You look very well, Isabella,' said Lady Beverley, smiling mistily on her daughter. 'Do not forget, you hold our fortune in your hands.'

Isabella reflected, as Mr Judd led her out to his carriage five minutes later, that she had not really used the viscount properly in learning how to flirt. She always felt too much at home with him to play games.

She was about to compliment Mr Judd on his carriage and horses and stopped herself in time. Both carriage and horses had recently been the pride and joy of the Beverleys.

She noticed uneasily that there was no footman or groom on the backstrap, not even a tiger, but she composed herself. Mr Judd drove very fast indeed and so conversation was impossible as the first few miles flashed past. When he slowed at last, Isabella said, 'This is not the road to Hedgefield.'

'Thought I'd show off a little first,' he said with that foxy grin of his. 'What think you of my driving, hey?'

'I think you a capital whip, sir,' lied Isabella.

'Oh, I'm a goer all right. Can drive to an inch. You see those gateposts?' He pointed with his whip at an open farm gate some distance away, situated at a bend in the road.

'Yes, Mr Judd.'

'Now you would think that too narrow for me to get through.'

'Yes, indeed.'

'Well, watch this.'

'Really, Mr Judd, I do not believe—' But the rest of Isabella's words were lost as he whipped up his horses, who surged down the road towards the gate, the carriage bumping crazily over the ruts. Isabella hung on tightly and closed her eyes. There was a splintering sound. She opened her eyes. The horses were rearing and plunging and the carriage was stuck fast in the gate.

'Shite!' shouted Mr Judd, his face red with fury. He jumped down, took out a knife and cut the traces and led the horses off into the field. Unless I marry him and control him, thought Isabella desperately, he will ruin everything that is Mannerling – temple, trees, horses, and carriages.

He wandered around the field, kicking the turf savagely, then he returned ill-tempered to where Isabella sat in the ruined carriage. 'Sorry about that,' he said sulkily. 'Was thinking of another gate. That's it. Another one down the road.'

'Of course,' said Isabella calmly.

'You'd best stay put and I'll ride one of these beasts to Hedgefield and get help.'

'Very well, sir,' said Isabella. The sun was becoming quite hot. She unfurled her parasol. Mr Judd walked away and swung himself up onto the back of one of the horses and rode off over the field away from the gate.

After some time, Isabella found sitting in a sloping carriage which was resting on its poles too uncomfortable. She climbed down, took off her pelisse and spread it on the grass and sat down and waited.

And waited.

* * *

Mr Judd went to the inn at Hedgefield and sent an ostler to find someone to collect the carriage and take it away for repair. He decided to have a glass of something cool in the tap to refresh himself before returning to Isabella.

It was then he saw a group of men at a table by the window playing cards. His eyes lit up. Since his magnificent win of Mannerling, he had vowed never to touch a card again. He had seen too many lose all they had won because of an inability to stop. But this was country cards and these were country yokels. Just one hand and then he would return to Isabella. He strolled over and as he did so one man threw down his cards in disgust and said, 'I'd best be off. Dame Fortune don't smile on me today.' Mr Judd slid into the vacated place and smiled all around. 'Mind if I join you?'

They mumbled that they did not. He gave a happy little sigh and concentrated on the game. By the second game he had forgotten about Isabella. By the third game, when the ostler returned to say that the blacksmith was gone from home and would not be back until five, Mr Judd only said vaguely, 'Oh, ah, well, fetch him when you can,' and with his green eyes gleaming, returned to the game.

Now what do I do? wondered Isabella. The sun was very hot indeed, and Mr Judd had not returned. She felt she was perfectly capable of sitting astride one of the remaining horses and riding home, but her skirt would ride up and she would present an undignified spectacle. But as another hot hour passed, enlivened only by the hum of insects and the sounds of larks in the clear sky above, she began to become increasingly angry. In these wicked days, it was shabby treatment to leave an unprotected female alone in the country-side. If Mr Judd had not found anyone to help, then he should have ridden back to tell her so. She walked to the far end of the field. Why, there was Hedgefield, just across the fields, only a few miles away. Where on earth was the man?

She was just walking back when she heard the sound of a carriage on the road and ran back towards the gate where Mr Judd's broken carriage was still lodged. She leaned over the fence beside the carriage.

Lord Fitzpatrick in a light gig pulled by one horse came driving round the bend. He saw Isabella and pulled at the reins to stop his horse and then jumped down and ran back to her.

He looked at the jammed carriage, at the three horses cropping grass in the field, and then at Isabella's flushed and miserable face.

'Judd, I suppose.'

'Yes, how did you know?'

'I do not think anyone else in the county would treat either carriage or horses so, not to mention a beautiful lady. Trying to show off, was he?'

'Yes, he said he could drive through the gateposts and as you can see, he could not. I have been here for *hours*, my lord. May I beg you to take me home?'

'You do not even need to beg.' He reached over the fence and caught her round the waist and lifted her, parasol and all, lightly over and set her down on the road.

'Do you think something might have befallen him?' asked Isabella.

'Unless he is dead, there is no excuse. He could easily have sent someone out from the town to help you or hired a horse and gig to pick you up.'

He lifted her into the gig, as easily, thought Isabella, as he would a doll.

'It is as well I came along,' he said, picking up the reins. 'You might have got a soaking to add to your misery.'

'On this sunny day?'

He pointed over to the west. 'Look!'

Black clouds were boiling up towards the sun and then, as she looked, she heard a faint rumble of thunder. She gave a little shiver.

'Not cold, surely, Miss Isabella?'

'No, no, it's just that an approaching thunderstorm now seems like a bad omen. The last one was when I arrived back at Mannerling to hear Papa had lost everything.' She remembered vividly the white faces of her sisters in the gloom as they listened to Mr Ducket outlining the extent of the Beverley losses in his precise voice.

'We will soon be home.'

'What brought you here, my lord?'

'I was taking some of my aunt's cordial to a sick cottager who lives quite near here.'

'But not on your estate!'

'My aunt's kindness knows no boundaries, believe

me. Now what would you have me do? After I leave you, shall I ride to Hedgefield and punch Mr Judd's nose for you?'

'Oh, no,' exclaimed Isabella. 'I am sure there is some perfectly reasonable explanation for the delay.'

He looked at her sharply. 'It would be folly should any member of your family think that marriage to such as Judd would reclaim Mannerling.'

Isabella lowered her parasol to shield her face. 'We all still miss Mannerling quite dreadfully, but thanks to Mrs Kennedy's kindness and efficiency, we are learning to adjust ourselves to our new fortunes.'

'Good. Would you care for another ride on Satan?'

'Oh, yes, please. But not today, surely.'

'Tomorrow at three will do very well, provided the weather is clement. I shall ask your father's permission.'

To the viscount's surprise, they were greeted on the doorstep by the Beverley family, mother, father, and Isabella's sisters, all crying out questions as to why she had not returned with Mr Judd. He did not know that they had not been worried about Isabella, thinking her long absence boded well for a forthcoming marriage. They had heard the carriage and had all come out to welcome Mr Judd.

Before Isabella could say anything, the viscount was giving them a succinct account of how he had found Isabella abandoned in a country field, where she had been waiting for hours.

'Poor Mr Judd,' said Sir William to the viscount's amazement. 'Something dire must have befallen him.

I shall send Barry over to Hedgefield to find out what happened.'

Rain was beginning to fall in fat, warm drops. 'No, that will not be necessary,' said Isabella quickly, appalled at the idea of sending Barry out in a storm and not realizing how much she had changed in that she was actually thinking of the well-being of a servant.

Barry himself came up at that moment and suggested he stable the viscount's horse and carriage until the storm passed, but the viscount said that a little rain would not hurt him and that he must return to his aunt, and after having secured permission to go riding with Isabella the following day, he made his goodbyes.

The fact was that he found he disliked and despised Sir William and did not want to spend any time with him.

A flash of lightning lit up the sky and the rain came down in sheets. Mr Judd gave an exclamation and threw down his cards. It was not Isabella who rushed back into his mind but the welfare of his horses left in the field.

The blacksmith had been waiting for an hour for him with several men who were to drive out and collect the carriage for repair.

Mr Judd had to offer them extra payment, then he had to pay for the hire of a gig to drive out to rescue Isabella. Before he left the inn, he asked if Mr Ducket was still in residence, for he wanted to enlist his help for the ball at Mannerling, but he was told that the secretary had left.

When he arrived at the field, he saw through the sheets of driving rain that Isabella had gone. He rapped out instructions about the carriage. Then the three carriage horses were tied to the back of the gig and he set out for Mannerling. Once there, he quickly dried and changed and called for a closed carriage to be ready and waiting. Then he set out for Brookfield House, rehearsing excuses.

The rain had not stopped, although the thunder had ceased to roll. He climbed down from the carriage, telling his servants to wait.

He walked from the carriage, which he had ordered to stop at the gates, up the short drive. He saw that the lamps in the downstairs parlour had been lit, and through a gap in the curtains, which were not quite drawn across, he saw the Beverley family. The sash window was raised at the bottom, for the night was muggy and close. He heard his name. Instead of knocking at the door, he edged along to that window and listened.

'No sign yet of Mr Judd.' That was Isabella's clear voice. 'I do really think that perhaps Barry should go to Hedgefield after all and find out what happened to him.'

'I think,' said the youngest sister, Lizzie, 'that there is no excuse for Mr Judd's behaviour. He could have sent someone out from Hedgefield to rescue Isabella even if he could not go himself. *I* think he is a shabby fellow and not a patch on Lord Fitzpatrick.'

Now Lady Beverley's voice, cold and haughty. 'You forget. Isabella is to reclaim Mannerling for us.'

'By marrying such a man?' Lizzie's voice was sharp.

'Oh, do not go on, Lizzie,' said Isabella. 'I am supposed to marry someone, so it may as well be Mr Judd.'

'May as well be Mr Judd!' echoed Lady Beverley scornfully. 'It is Isabella's duty to sacrifice herself. Something must be done to stop the wretched man from ruining Mannerling with his vulgar ruins and horrible alterations.'

Mr Judd retreated from the window and stood gnawing at his knuckles. And to think he had rather fancied that Isabella bitch! And yet she was so very beautiful. He had imagined taking her to London and being the envy of all the fellows. Black anger was rising up in him, but he put on his gambler's poker face and went and knocked at the door.

Betty answered it but he did not wait for her to announce him, pushing rudely past the girl and walking straight into the parlour.

How well they did it, what an act, he thought as they clustered about him without one word of recrimination, all asking questions about his welfare.

'I regret to say that a bolt of lightning struck me,' he said, holding on to a chairback for support. 'I was knocked unconscious. The physician said it was a miracle I was not struck dead. Imagine my horror when I regained my senses to remember with my first waking thought poor Miss Isabella. "Do not move," they cried, but I was determined. I rode hell for leather back to the field and found Miss Isabella gone. I came straight here.'

'Do sit down, Mr Judd. Betty, fetch the brandy,' said Lady Beverley. The sisters, with the exception of Isabella, murmured little sympathetic noises. But the storm did not break until after I had been in that field for hours, thought Isabella. And if he rushed straight here, then how is it he has changed his clothes?

Her heart felt heavy and she became aware that the rest were darting anxious little looks in her direction. She forced herself to ask solicitously after his welfare. They all fussed about him, placing him in the best chair by the fire, finding him a footstool for his feet, and putting a silk cushion behind his head.

'So how did you get home, Miss Isabella?' he finally asked, those odd light-green eyes of his fixed on her face.

'Lord Fitzpatrick came by and drove me here,' said Isabella.

'Fitzpatrick, hey? I sent him an invitation to call, which he refused. Who does he think he is, hey? But he'll come to my ball. They'll all come to Mannerling for a ball.'

Lady Beverley gave a little preliminary cough. 'I would like to offer my services to you, Mr Judd. We have given many balls at Mannerling and I am accounted a fine hostess.'

'No need for that,' he said, 'Miss Isabella here can give me any advice I need.' He was beginning to enjoy the comedy, to enjoy the triumphant exchange of glances that this last statement had caused.

'I should consider myself honoured,' said Isabella politely.

Mr Judd said he could do with some help in drawing up the invitation list. He had meant to ask Mr Ducket, but they had told him at the inn at Hedgefield that Mr Ducket had left. 'We can start now,' said Isabella. She produced sheets of paper and a lead pencil and then Lady Beverley began to tell her which names to write down. To Mr Judd's malicious and secret glee, Lady Beverley began to forget that it was not she who was giving the ball and said things like, 'I suppose we shall have to ask the Tomneys, although they are really quite common and the daughter is a hoyden; and put down the Franks, unexceptionable, although I believe she drinks.'

Look at 'em, marvelled Mr Judd, lost their house and lost their lands and pretty much all of their possessions and yet as proud and haughty as ever.

Well, well, pride could be lost, too, and he, Ajax Judd, was going to see to that!

FIVE

Better be courted and jilted
Than never be courted at all

THOMAS CAMPBELL

Isabella looked foward to her ride with the viscount.
There was nothing to worry her there. She could be
herself, be easy and friendly, not try to pretend to
like a man she secretly despised. For she was now
honest enough to admit to herself that she did not
particularly like Mr Judd. But she lived in a world
where ladies of the ton married men every day whom
they did not particularly like – because families or
lawyers or both had arranged the match, or simply
because a lady just *had* to get married. And as the
eldest sister, she felt the pressure from the others to
get them back their home.

Mrs Kennedy arrived with the viscount in separate
carriages, with Satan tied to the viscount's curricle,
which was a signal for Lady Beverley to retire to her
bedchamber with a headache. Secretly she blamed her
husband for all the indignities that had been heaped on
her head, and Lady Beverley considered the affection

with which even Jessica had begun to greet the arrival of Mrs Kennedy just one of those indignities.

She did not object to Isabella's riding out with the viscount. She felt that perhaps Mr Judd might be spurred to warmer behaviour if he thought he had a rival.

The day was fresh and windy, with great white clouds tumbling across the sky. Isabella praised Mrs Kennedy's needlework to her nephew and the viscount laughed and said if they ever lost all their money, he was sure his aunt could support him by turning professional dressmaker. Then he said, 'And what of Judd? What had befallen him?'

'Mr Judd said he had been struck by lightning and passed out.'

'But you had been there for ages when I found you and the storm had not yet started!'

'That is what he says and I must believe him.'

'Why?'

'It would be impolite to do otherwise.'

'And did Sir William and Lady Beverley give him his character for having abandoned their daughter?'

'They could hardly do that when the contrite gentleman came straight to Brookfield to give his apologies and say he had been struck by lightning.'

'His clothes all charred?'

'He had his evening clothes on.'

'Hardly the young Lochinvar riding directly to his lady's side.'

'Let us not talk about him. Have you received a call from our good vicar?'

'Ah, Mr Stoppard and his daughter Mary. Yes, they called several times.'

'They have not called on us once,' said Isabella bitterly.

'That was always the way of toad-eaters. Talking of toad-eaters, have you ever seen one of those mountebanks' creatures actually eat a toad?'

'Once, when I was small, when our nurse took us to the fair. She lost her employ with us because of it.'

Their horses were ambling slowly together under the trees. Isabella still vividly remembered that day. Mountebanks and their toad-eaters were popular figures. After the toad-eater had swallowed a toad and slumped to the boards of the mountebank's stage, the mountebank or quack would force a cure-all through the supposedly dying lips of the toad-eater, who would then leap to his feet. The mountebank would then make his way through the crowd, selling his cure-all to the gullible. Isabella remembered standing in the crowd watching the performance, remembered how frightened they had all been of the noise and jostling of the fair, of the crowd of ballad singers, bear wards, geomancers, hocus-pocus men, jugglers, mandrake men, merry andrews, puppet masters, rope dancers, tooth drawers, and tumblers. How on their return to the cool elegance of Mannerling they had told their mother of the visit to the fair, how Lady Beverley's thin lips had folded into an even thinner line, and how the old nurse had been sent packing. And she remembered the nurse's tears and her own guilt, knowing somehow that the

95

nurse had only sought to entertain them and that they should not have complained.

'Why on earth did she lose her job with you?' she realized the viscount was asking.

She gave a weak smile and said, 'Visits to fairs were not approved of by my parents.'

'And did you terrifying children subsequently get rid of any governess who did not please you?'

Isabella bit her lip. 'Such governesses as we have had, and the one Lizzie and the twins had before we moved to Brookfield, were sad, respectable creatures. I sometimes fret that our schooling has been genteel rather than educational, but after what happened to Nurse, we all made sure we did not complain. What can such women do if they are turned off without a reference?'

'And yet turned off they were, for you said "governesses."'

'Ah, well, as to that, Mama would meet someone at a rout or ball who would puff themselves up over the accomplishments of their daughters, accomplishments we did not excel in, such as water-colour painting or pianoforte playing, and so another governess had to be found to compete. But Mama always thought she was doing the best for us,' added Isabella loyally.

'You do not seem to have had a normal childhood. Did you not play in the stables or the hayloft or get up to any mischief?'

Isabella gave a little sigh. 'I suppose we did not. It was always borne in us that we were ladies of fortune and rank and must always speak in low voices, never show vulgar animation, and yet we were happy. We had Mannerling, you see.'

And Mannerling, he thought, became substitute for human love and affection.

He felt he should begin to back away from her and not get too close. If he married her, then he would have the weight of the Beverley family around his neck. The first thing that selfish old charlatan, Sir William, would want him to do would be to buy back Mannerling from Judd, which of course he would not. Then he had to think more clearly about Isabella's character and not be blinded by her beauty. Perhaps the damage had already been done and she could never love anyone better than she loved Mannerling.

'Let's gallop,' he said abruptly. They spurred their horses and side by side raced down the bridle-path and out into the open country. Isabella felt a sudden rush of freedom and joy, as if she were flying away from all her cares – from Mr Judd, from the almost constant shadow of the Beverleys's ruin.

The great horse surged under her as if infected by her gladness. With a feeling of triumph, she came abreast of the viscount and they hurtled out of the trees and across the fields, finally coming to a stop where the fields met the Hedgefield road.

'Bravo!' he cried. 'You ride well.'

Isabella glowed with pleasure, her eyes meeting his in open friendship. 'Let us ride on to the Green Man,' he said, 'and have something to drink.'

They cantered into Hedgefield and into the court-yard of the inn.

He lifted her down from the saddle and she lowered her eyelashes and turned slightly pink as she felt the pressure of his hands at her waist.

He looked at her quizzically as he led her into the inn, at her averted face.

But when they were seated and sharing a jug of lemonade, she appeared to recover her composure. She was beginning to chat happily about the fine points of Satan when the vicar and his daughter walked into the tap.

'Oh, Miss Beverley,' cooed Mary, stopping by their table and dropping a curtsy. 'Have you seen Mr Judd?'

'No,' said Isabella. The landlord came into the tap at that moment and the vicar called to him, 'Have you seen Mr Judd of Mannerling?'

'Not since yesterday,' said the landlord. 'He was playing cards here all afternoon.'

'You cannot mean Mr Judd,' exclaimed Isabella. 'He was struck by lightning, was he not?'

The landlord scratched his head. 'Reckon I would ha' heard of that, had it happened.'

'What gave you such a *quaint* notion!' declared Mary.

Stiff-necked pride stopped Isabella from saying that it was none other than Mr Judd himself who had told her so. The viscount, to her relief, remained silent. Mary's black eyes darted from one to the other. Then she said, 'We have received our invitations to the ball at Mannerling.'

Isabella felt another shock go through her. No invitations had arrived at Brookfield House. 'Of course,'

Mary went on, 'it will not be so *grand* as it was in Sir William's day.'

'Do not let us keep you,' said the viscount in a flat voice.

'Oh . . . yes, we will be on our way,' said Mr Stoppard hurriedly. 'I shall be calling on you soon, Lord Fitzpatrick.'

'Pray do not. Mrs Kennedy, my aunt, is not in the best of health and we do not wish visitors.'

'In that case, we will eagerly await her recovery,' said the vicar, a red spot on each cheek. He recognized a snub, and so he should, thought Isabella bitterly. He had already had a long life of toadying and must have become used to it.

'Dreadful people,' murmured the viscount, and despite her distaste for them, Isabella was surprised at the extent of her own dislike. The toadying Stoppards had been so much part of the Mannerling life that until the Fall, as she called their ruin to herself, she had taken such grovelling adulation as her due. Again a picture of Mr Judd rose up in her mind. To go to such lengths for such a man! And then she was suddenly impatient with the viscount's company, for it was surely his company which was making her lose sight of her objective.

The viscount watched amused as different emotions followed each other on Isabella's face like cloud shadows crossing a field.

He suddenly thought with a tug at his heart that if she would forget about Mannerling completely, if he could be sure of that, then he would ask her to marry him. Certainly the Beverleys in their pride had warned him off, but their circumstances were different now and they could not afford to be so choosey.

John, the footman from Mannerling, stood over in a corner with a tankard of shrub and covertly watched the couple. He was anxious to ingratiate himself with his master, Mr Judd, who was threatening to turn him into a hermit. The gossip among the Mannerling servants was that Mr Judd would marry Miss Isabella Beverley. Did Mr Judd know of the courtship of Lord Fitzpatrick? Besides, such a piece of gossip might make Mr Judd lose interest in this eldest Beverley daughter and that might be all to the good. Too many of the servants had shown their open dislike of the Beverleys, their lack of sympathy for the family's plight. If Isabella were to become mistress of Mannerling, she might persuade her husband to get rid of them all and hire new ones.

He slid quietly out before the couple could see him. He had been sent to check on how the repairs to the carriage were coming along and had already done that. So he rode back to Mannerling and asked the butler if he might see Mr Judd in private. The butler, Chubb, frowned and said anything that had to be said to the master must be said through him, and so John retreated, balked. But he waited for an opportune moment, which came in the early evening, when he saw Mr Judd walking in the grounds smoking a cheroot.

He darted out of the door and approached him. 'Sir,' he began, coming up to him.

Mr Judd swung round, his eyes narrowing as he observed his least favourite footman.

'I have come by some intelligence that may amaze you,' said John pompously.

'I doubt it.' Mr Judd dropped his smouldering cheroot on the lawn and ground it in with his heel.

'I saw Miss Isabella Beverley in the Green Man with Lord Fitzpatrick.'

Mr Judd looked at his footman with narrowed eyes. 'And what's that to do with me, popinjay?'

'Well, sir, they were very *close*, if you take my meaning. All alone, too. No maid or footman.'

Mr Judd strode away and John tittuped after him on his high heels.

The master of Mannerling was thinking furiously. This was not working out as he had planned. He must behave in a warmer manner towards Isabella. He had deliberately not sent out the Beverleys's invitation to his ball so as to 'make them sweat a bit,' as he maliciously put it to himself.

He stopped so abruptly that John nearly cannoned into him. 'You can be of use to me,' said Mr Judd. 'I want you to go direct to Brookfield House. I found the Beverleys's invitations still on my desk. Take the carriage. I want you to bring Miss Isabella back with you . . . for dinner. I will write a letter.'

He strode off towards the house, with the footman mincing after him.

Isabella and the viscount rode easily and companionably back to Brookfield House. For the time being,

Isabella had forgotten about Mr Judd and about her ambition to marry him. But Lady Beverley herself came out to meet her daughter. 'Do come into the house immediately, Isabella,' she cried. 'We have such news.'

The viscount dismounted and lifted Isabella down under the hard stare of Lady Beverley's disapproving eyes. 'Perhaps Lord Fitzpatrick would care to step inside for a glass of wine,' said Isabella.

'Oh, I am sure he has much to attend to,' said Lady Beverley hurriedly.

Isabella turned red with mortification at her mother's rudeness. The viscount swung himself easily into his curricle, touched his hat, and rode off, with Satan following behind.

'How could you?' fumed Isabella as she followed her mother into the house. 'How rude! And after all Lord Fitzpatrick's kindness.'

'Never mind that,' said Lady Beverley eagerly. 'You must get changed and put on one of your prettiest gowns. The Mannerling carriage is round the back, with John, the footman, waiting for you. You are to go to dinner at Mannerling!'

Isabella stood stock-still in the dark hall. In her mind's eye another Isabella raced away across the fields on Satan's back, happy and free.

'And he has sent the invitations to his ball with such a pretty note of apology saying he had found them down the back of his desk. Good heavens, child, do not stand there as if you had been struck by lightning like Mr Judd. Bustle about!'

'Mr Judd was not struck by lightning,' said Isabella flatly. 'He was playing cards in the Green Man yesterday.'

'What? Oh, why are we wasting time? Betty! Betty! Come and see to your mistress and get a good gown on. You are to go to Mannerling with Miss Isabella!'

Isabella sat in the Mannerling carriage an hour later, scented and pomaded and wearing a heavy gold silk dinner gown. Betty covertly watched Isabella's sad face and wondered not for the first time why miss did not settle for the handsome viscount instead of wasting time with such a dreadful man as Mr Judd.

The weather had changed again, to match Isabella's mood. Rain pattered on the roof of the carriage, and as they turned in at the gates of Mannerling, the wind rose in a great gust which sounded like an enormous sigh.

Isabella wondered if Mrs Judd disapproved of her or if that lady had a perpetually sour air and expression. Conversation during dinner was extremely stilted. Mrs Judd complained about the size of Mannerling and the uppitiness of the servants. Mr Judd ate great quantities of food and occasionally broke off from eating to pay Isabella a heavy compliment which did not please her. She wished he would not speak with his mouth full or declare that the best way to eat peas was with a knife smeared in butter, and only man-milliners chased them around the plate with a two-pronged fork.

I am going to marry this man, thought Isabella bleakly, and therefore this will be just the first of many

103

such evenings. But Mrs Judd would not stay in residence, and surely he would let her family move back with her.

After dinner, in the drawing room, Mr Judd asked her to play something on the pianoforte. Isabella obediently sat down to play, her fingers rippling over the keys, her back to the room, dreaming that when she finished playing and turned round, all would be as it had once been. But when she finally finished playing and turned around, it was to find that both Mr Judd and his mother were sprawled in their chairs, fast asleep.

She longed to escape. All she had to do was to summon Betty and the carriage, slip out quietly and go home. But, in a way, to do that would be to give up the battle, to admit to herself that she did not want to marry Mr Judd, and that would mean giving up any hope of Mannerling, Mannerling which was changing daily as Mr Judd brought in more ugly furniture and paintings and planned to desecrate the grounds.

She turned back to the keys and began to play a noisy piece with many crashing chords, so that when she finally finished and turned back, both were awake.

'Jolly good,' said Mr Judd, stifling a yawn.

'I prefer pretty ballads myself,' said Mrs Judd. 'Miss Stoppard, now, does play some pretty tunes.'

'You are tired and it is late,' said Isabella. 'I thank you for a most pleasant evening.'

When a footman announced the carriage had been brought round, Isabella was accompanied down the stairs and outside by Mr Judd. He said to Betty, 'Get in the carriage. Your mistress will follow in a few moments.'

He turned and smiled down at Isabella with his foxy smile. 'I'm tired o' the single life. Got an important announcement to make at the ball, so look your finest.'

Isabella blushed modestly and looked down. He tilted her face up and gave her a quick hard kiss on the lips. 'So no more jauntering about the countryside with Fitzpatrick, hey?'

'As you wish,' said Isabella, the picture of meek womanhood.

'Good girl. Be calling soon.'

He handed Isabella into the carriage. She smiled at him sweetly. The coachman cracked his whip and the carriage rolled off.

Now all Isabella felt was sweet triumph. She had done it, by God! She was no longer a failure. Then she remembered promising to ride out with the viscount in two days' time. Well, Barry would need to go over to Perival and say she was indisposed.

When she told her family her news, she basked in their admiration. Lady Beverley began to plan the wedding. Jessica was in alt. Isabella was the cleverest of sisters, and they had never doubted for a moment that she could rescue them. Only Lizzie suddenly said in a lull in all the congratulations, 'Will you be happy, Isabella?'

Isabella fought down a sudden qualm and said brightly, 'Of course. I will be back at Mannerling. I will be *home* again.'

* * *

Although Isabella made excuses not to go riding with the viscount again, she found it hard to keep to her room, supposedly ill, when Mrs Kennedy came calling. For her sisters were enjoying their cooking and sewing lessons, and so had no reason to give them up. Isabella could hardly be said to be encouraging the attentions of the viscount, and so Mrs Kennedy would have no reason to feel angry when Isabella's engagement to Mr Judd was announced at the Mannerling ball.

Also, Isabella found the days long, and time lay heavy on her hands. Mr Judd took her driving several times and sent her presents of flowers and hothouse fruit, but he hardly seemed like the ardent lover. On their last drive out he had said he would now be busy right up until the ball, but when her hopes flagged a little, he gave her his sly sideways smile and said the announcement would be worth waiting for.

One day, a week before the Mannerling ball, she learned that Mrs Kennedy was not to call that day and so she wandered out into the garden to find Barry. He was working on building a hen-run. She stood for a few moments watching him and then joined him.

Suddenly eager to confide in someone other than the members of her family, she said, 'Mr Judd is to announce his engagement to me at the Mannerling ball next week, Barry.'

'There now,' he said slowly. 'There be a thing I did not rightly expect.'

'And why not?'

106

'To be sure, miss, I had been thinking that perhaps you and that Lord Fitzpatrick might make a go of it.'

'No, no, Barry. You must be happy for me. You see, I will soon be back in my old home.'

He looked distressed. 'But it can hardly be the same, miss, what with you becoming Mrs Judd and all.'

'How will that make any difference?'

He looked at her innocent eyes and shook his head. 'Not my place to say, miss.'

He watched her sadly as she walked away. Isabella could feel her courage ebbing each step she took away from him. But she was doing the *right* thing. It was her *duty* to reclaim Mannerling.

But she could not bear to return to the house and face the others. She walked away over the fields, feeling the strengthening breeze tugging at her muslin skirts. She took off her straw bonnet and let it dangle by the satin ribbons from her hand. She had gone quite a bit away from the house and was enjoying the fresh air and exercise, feeling her courage coming back, when she heard the thud of horses' hoofs across the turf and, looking up, saw, with a sinking heart, the viscount riding towards her. He reined in and dismounted and looked at her thoughtfully.

'You do not look at all unwell to me,' he said abruptly.

'I am recovered,' said Isabella, turning her face away and looking out across the fields.

He eyed her impatiently. He had missed her more than he wanted to admit to himself. She looked even more beautiful to him with her hair tousled by the wind and the skirts of her thin gown blowing about her than when she was coiffed and groomed.

And then, all at once, he knew he wanted her more than anything in the world.

'Miss Isabella,' he said in a rush. 'Will you marry me?'

She turned to him, shocked and alarmed.

'I cannot!'

'May I know why?'

She blurted out, 'I am to marry Mr Judd. He is to make an announcement at the ball next week.'

His face darkened with fury and she backed away a step.

'Do not look at me like that, my lord. You know what my old home means to me.'

'And what does this Judd mean to you? Good God, have you thought you will need to entertain him in your bed?'

Eyes of puzzled innocence stared into his own.

'You do not know what I am talking about,' he jeered. 'But you soon will, and God help you.'

Her lips quivered and tears filled her eyes.

He gave a stifled exclamation and pulled her roughly into his arms and kissed her, at first angrily, and then very gently. Then he mounted his horse and rode off without looking back.

She stood in the field, her hand to her mouth, and watched him go.

Then she suddenly sat down and began to cry as she had not cried since she had been a child.

After some time, she slowly recovered. Across the

fields came the old familiar pull of Mannerling, calling her home.

She regretted losing the viscount's friendship. He should not have kissed her, and yet she could still feel that second kiss, that gentle one, warm against her lips.

Isabella began to walk home, trying to think only of Mannerling, trying to think only of what it would be like to be home again until Mr Judd, that instrument of bringing it all about, had sunk back to a shadowy and unthreatening figure in her mind.

Mrs Kennedy looked up with a sigh of relief as her nephew strode into the dining room that evening. She rang a little bell beside her plate as a signal that the meal could now be served. But her relief soon changed to anxiety. She had never before seen him look so drawn or grim.

'Faith, what's amiss?' she cried.

He sat down heavily and ran his fingers through his thick hair. 'What a day,' he muttered.

'So what happened?'

His eyes signalled that the servants were entering carrying the dinner. Mrs Kennedy had to content herself by talking in generalities, in talking about the Beverleys and what a pity it was that poor Miss Isabella was unwell, and about what progress the others were making with their sewing, all the time fretting and fretting about the dark look in her nephew's eyes.

At last, when the covers had been cleared and the decanters brought in and bowls of fruit and nuts shone on the polished surface of the mahogany table, Mrs Kennedy nodded to the servants to leave and turned anxiously to the viscount. 'So now tell me – what has happened?'

'I was fool enough to propose marriage to Miss Isabella Beverley.'

Mrs Kennedy raised her little chubby hands in a gesture of amazement. 'Never say she turned you down.'

'She not only turned me down but told me that she is to marry Judd.'

'Why? He's a repulsive creature.'

'Because of Mannerling. Because anyone Irish is still not good enough for the Beverleys. Because she is willing to sacrifice herself for a pile of bricks and mortar. The announcement is to be made at the ball.'

Mrs Kennedy felt her temper rising. She had, on a couple of occasions, overheard Jessica mimicking her accent but had good-naturedly said nothing about it, considering that it would take some time for the proud Beverleys to appreciate their changed circumstances.

'So Isabella has not been ill?'

The viscount shook his head.

'We made a mistake being friendly with such people. By all that's holy,' said Mrs Kennedy wrathfully, 'you would wonder what more is needed to bring that stiff-necked family to its senses. They may rot in hell. I shan't go there anymore. It's Isabella I'm disappointed in. Lying and pretending she was ill. I thought she had more character than the rest. I'm not angry at her turning you down, it's the reason that makes me

110

fair boil. I hope that spalpeen, Judd, gets drunk one night, knocks over his bed candle and sets the whole place up, wit' himself inside.' Her accent became broader in her anger. 'A fellow straight out o' the bogs o' Kilkenny has more dignity than that lot! And you can tear up our invitations to the ball.'

The viscount poured them each a glass of port. 'We shall go. I shall look at the joy and gratification on the faces of those Beverleys and my heart will be eased by thinking that I have had a lucky escape. But, oh, she is so very beautiful.'

'Humph! Beauty don't last. I remember Colonel Petrey's lady. Like a picture she was wit' these great blue eyes and a little neat figure and ankles to die for. When her looks began to go, she became petulant, and the more her looks faded, the more she flirted outrageously wit' every man in the regiment, so she did, all trying to bolster her vanity. Ended up a semi-invalid, dosing herself with rubbish in a darkened room, and all because she could no longer face the world. Go for character, and that don't mean any of those Beverley girls.' Her eyes filled with tears. 'And I thought they liked me.'

'I am sure they do,' he said quietly, 'and they will miss you and missing you will do them no harm at all. Drink your port, Aunt Mary.'

And although the Beverley sisters spent their time looking forward to the ball and anticipating Isabella's triumph, they did miss Mrs Kennedy. Only Isabella knew the reason for her absence, the reason for the

111

curt letter that lady had sent saying she would be too much occupied in the following days and weeks to call on them and too busy to receive them. She had not told her family of the viscount's proposal. Lizzie, who had been making new curtains for the parlour under Mrs Kennedy's tuition, felt lost and bewildered. She had begun to look forward to each visit of the Irishwoman. She no longer had a governess and time lay heavy on her hands. Sharper than the rest, she suspected that somehow Isabella had ruined the friendship. Mrs Kennedy must be mad with Isabella, for Isabella had pretended to be ill and Lizzie was sure Mrs Kennedy had not been deceived by the excuses, not knowing that the good-hearted lady had believed every word of them until her nephew had opened her eyes.

Jessica, the proudest of them all, struggled with an uneasy conscience. She had been doing an imitation of Mrs Kennedy one day when she had suddenly turned and had seen that lady standing in the doorway. Jessica had had the grace to blush but Mrs Kennedy had gone on in her usual friendly way and so Jessica had comforted herself with the thought that she might not have heard anything. She had the sense to admit reluctantly to herself that she had taken Mrs Kennedy's great kindness for granted and she felt shabby. But like the rest, she clung to the thought of returning to Mannerling. They would probably not be able to live there once Isabella was married, but they could go over on visits every day if they liked.

Isabella had many ball gowns which had been made for her London Season and had not yet been seen in the country. She now did not regret the loss of her jewels. She had always felt uneasily, when they were all decked out like barbaric princesses, that it was a trifle vulgar.

Barry had hired a carriage for the evening and would wear a suit of dark clothes and act as footman. Betty would act as lady's-maid. Nothing could go wrong now. All they had to do was wait for the great day.

SIX

Gunpowder, Treason and Plot.

ANONYMOUS

It was the great day at last, bright, calm, and fair. There was to be a full moon.

Betty, running from one sister to the other, reflected that they had all forgotten she was merely an ordinary maid as each commandeered her attention as if she were that sister's own private lady's-maid. It was Isabella who finally put a stop to it and told her sisters that they were supposed to be able now to look after themselves and it was too much work for Betty. She ordered Betty to the kitchen and told her to ask Joshua to make her tea and then informed her sisters that she would arrange their hair herself. Isabella was glad of the occupation. For some reason all the elation she had felt at her 'triumph' was ebbing away and she heartily wished the evening were over.

The house was full of the smells of perfume, pomade, and hot hair. Isabella wielded the curling-tongs to such good effect that her sisters declared she was better than any lady's-maid. She herself was wearing a muslin gown of dark rose, a break from the usual tradition of white muslin. Jessica was in pale green, Rachel and Abigail in lilac, Belinda in pink, and Lizzie in white. Their gowns, with the exception of Lizzie's, had been dyed and all had been altered to more stylish lines by Mrs Kennedy, and the sisters agreed that they looked all the crack; perhaps only Lizzie, in the excitement of all the preparations, remembering who was responsible for their very modish look.

They felt quite like their old selves as the Beverleys gathered in the drawing room for a glass of champagne before setting out for Mannerling. Isabella suddenly suggested that they should invite the servants in to share a glass and to wish them well. Lady Beverley looked outraged but the suggestion appealed to Sir William's gambling nature, and besides, he had come to believe that the ruin of the Beverleys was only a temporary hiccup in an otherwise pleasant life. Had he not that very day found a four-leafed clover in the garden by the hedge? Nothing could go wrong again.

And so the small band of servants was brought in. Barry toasted the family and wished them well, although in his heart of hearts he prayed that Isabella would never marry Mr Judd.

Some of the euphoria generated by the champagne faded a little as they climbed into the shabby rented carriage. Barry had had to scrub it out and remove every vestige of straw and it still smelled damp. They could not help thinking what sorry figures they would all cut arriving in such a rig.

But as they approached Mannerling, an almost hectic excitement invaded the party. They were going home.

Somehow they had expected the ball to be like one of their own, no expense spared. But there were no footmen in grand livery lining the staircase. Isabella thought that Mr Judd had probably sold those gold swords. Then there was no band from London but a few local men from Hedgefield to provide the music, which had a tinny, scraping sound. The walls were not hung with silk, nor were there any hothouse flowers. Mr Judd was standing at the top of the stairs beside his mother. Mrs Judd was dressed in unrelieved black. What had happened to all their jewels? wondered Isabella. She had braced herself to see Mrs Judd wearing some of them, but nothing glittered on any of that dull, depressing black.

The ballroom was full of familiar faces, all the people they used to invite themselves. Mary Stoppard was there wearing a silk gown with many tucks and gores and flounces. Her black eyes were gleaming with pleasure and Isabella noticed to her distress that it was Mary rather than Mrs Judd who kept an eye on the servants and who stopped at the entrance to the saloon where the refreshments were to be served to have a word with the butler. All that would soon change, she comforted herself.

And then hot colour flamed in her face as the viscount entered the room. For the first time, as her eyes went from Mr Judd to the viscount, she realized just how very attractive and handsome he was, how firm

116

his mouth . . . She remembered that kiss and blushed again. Mrs Kennedy went on as if every member of the Beverley family were invisible. Lizzie suppressed a shiver. Let the engagement be announced. Let everything be all right again, thought Isabella.

Mr Judd claimed her hand for the first dance. It was the quadrille. As they walked to join the others in a set, Mr Judd pressed her hand and said, 'Looking forward to the announcement?'

'Oh, yes,' said Isabella and gave him a wan smile.

He danced gawkily and badly, his legs flying out all over the place. He had remarkably thin shanks. The viscount had beautiful legs. Stop it! Stop it now! Isabella told her treacherous thoughts. She was glad when the dance was finally over and Mr Judd strolled off to claim another partner.

Then she found herself hoping that the viscount would ask her to dance, that he would forgive her, that he would say he understood why she must marry Mr Judd, but he did not come near her. She could not help noticing this time what a flutter he was causing among the young ladies.

She was sad that Mrs Kennedy had obviously decided the Beverleys were no longer worth knowing. And yet, little Lizzie, who spent most of the evening with the dowagers and chaperones, went and sat next to Mrs Kennedy. Mrs Kennedy turned her head away. Lizzie leaned forward and said something and Isabella saw Mrs Kennedy's face thaw somewhat and soon she appeared to be talking easily to Lizzie. At least she likes one of us, thought Isabella bleakly. She danced

117

and danced, wondering when that dreaded announcement would be made.

At last, just before the supper dance, Mr Judd
jumped up on the small dais in front of the band and
held up his hands.

'I have an important announcement to make,' he
said.

Everyone was suddenly very still and quiet, waiting.
Over, round and about them it was as if the very house
itself were waiting.

'I have great pleasure in announcing my engagement.'

There was a buzz of speculation. Isabella was aware
of many eyes on her. Mr Judd held up his hands again.

Mr Judd lowered his hands as he waited for the
silence to become absolute. Across the ballroom his
eyes met those of Isabella and he smiled, a slow, foxy
smile.

Then he said loudly and clearly, 'My intended is
none other than Miss Mary Stoppard, daughter of our
good vicar.'

Although Mr Judd held out a hand to Mary, who
was being led forward by her proud father, his eyes
never left Isabella's face. The stunned silence seemed
to go on and on.

The viscount was wondering whether to leap up
on the dais and punch Mr Judd on the nose. Isabella
deserved this, all of it, but how his heart ached for her!

And then Isabella gave a radiant smile and began
to clap. All around her people began to clap as well.
And then Isabella moved forward to the dais. She

gave Mary a hug and said, 'I am very happy for you, Mary. You and Mr Judd deserve each other.'

Mr Judd had a dark, baffled look on his face. The other Beverley sisters were crowding round, offering Mary their felicitations, their beautiful faces as radiant and happy as Isabella. The immense pride of the Beverleys had come to their rescue.

But this is not the end of it, thought Mr Judd, there's more to come, and their pride won't be able to stand another blow.

Footmen were circling the room with glasses of iced champagne. What a bunch of actresses, marvelled the viscount. And even Sir William and Lady Beverley were graciously smiling all about them, as if this were something they had already known about.

Again Mr Judd held up his hands for silence. 'I have another surprise. An entertainment. Everyone to the back terrace, please.'

Isabella muttered to her sisters as they made their way downstairs, 'Whatever happens, do not look distressed. Mr Judd is out to humiliate us.'

The guests crowded onto the back terrace, some of them spilling over into the garden, laughing and chatting, still carrying glasses of champagne.

Mr Judd, with Mary on his arm, waited until they were all assembled. It was a clear night, a full moon riding serenely overhead. The marble temple's white pillars gleamed across the vista of lawns and trees.

'What are we to watch?' cried someone. 'Fireworks?'

'In a way,' said Mr Judd, giving his foxy grin. 'Watch this!'

He took a large white handkerchief out of his pocket and waved it in the air.

A flicker of white over by the temple signalled a reply. In the bright moonlight, they could then see the little figure of a man running away from the temple.

And then there was a tremendous explosion. The temple flew apart, the roof blew right off and landed several yards away, the pillars shattered, and then black smoke obscured everything.

'What do you think?' chortled Mr Judd. 'Hated that thing.'

And then Dowager Lady Tarrant, whose house and lands lay on the far side of Hedgefield, said loudly and clearly, 'What disgusting desecration. I am going home. Someone get my carriage.'

Voices also calling for their carriages were raised all around. People were clustering around the Beverley family. Guests were murmuring to Sir William, 'The man is common, as common as dirt. We must exchange cards. We have not seen you this age.' One moment the terrace was full of people and then it seemed to the wrathful Mr Judd that they had all gone, gone even before supper, gone off into the night. Not one word of thanks, either, only cold, shocked silence.

The Beverleys walked to their shabby rented carriage. Word of Mr Judd's engagement and the ruin of the temple had spread like wildfire through the servants. Betty wrapped shawls about 'her ladies'' shoulders, Barry assisted them into the carriage as solemn and stately as the best of footmen.

Then they drove off, away from Mannerling. The air was full of the smell of gunpowder.

Jessica was the first to find her voice. 'That monster! But you misled us, Isabella. Mary Stoppard, mistress of Mannerling! It's beyond anything.'

'I see it now,' said Isabella in a tired voice. 'He led me to believe he would marry me. The disgusting man even kissed me. And all the time he was planning to humiliate me . . . us. Why? What did we ever do to incur such venom?'

Betty, the maid, crushed in a corner of the large, old, creaking carriage, said in a small voice, 'If I may make a suggestion, miss?'

'Go ahead,' said Isabella.

'The night of the storm,' said Betty, 'the night Lord Fitzpatrick found you left by Mr Judd and brought you home, I thought I heard a noise outside. I looked out and there was Mr Judd, listening at the parlour window.'

Isabella thought hard. 'Dear heavens, we were all discussing how I had to marry him to regain Mannerling. He must have heard. Betty, you silly widgeon, why did you not tell me?'

'It didn't seem my place, miss, and you did say you wasn't interested in servants' gossip. Besides, I did not know what you was saying in the parlour.'

'Gone,' said Sir William suddenly, 'all gone. But there is one last chance.'

The sisters looked at him wearily.

'What, Papa?' asked Isabella.

'I will tell you when we are home. Let us all have some tea in the drawing room. See to it, Betty.'

'Betty has done enough this evening,' declared Isabella quietly. 'One of the other maids can fetch it, or, if they are abed, then, wonder of wonders, one of the famous Beverleys might even know how to prepare a pot of tea with their very own useless hands.'

'Don't be vulgar,' admonished Jessica testily.

She was furious with Isabella. Somehow it was all Isabella's fault. She was not ruthless enough, nor brave enough. If Judd had heard them talking about him in the parlour, then he would have said something. No man would go to such lengths to humiliate them. He had said he did not like the temple. Isabella had probably been too vain to ever think he might prefer anyone else.

When they arrived home, Barry insisted on making the tea himself. He wanted an excuse to be in that drawing room when Sir William discussed this new plan, for Betty had whispered to him what Sir William had said in the carriage.

So when he carried the tea-things into the drawing room, he was just in time to hear Jessica ask, 'You said there was still hope, Papa. What do you mean? Judd is to marry the horrible Mary and I do not see how we can stop that.'

'Judd is a gambler and is bound to be out of funds soon,' said Sir William, a hectic light in his eyes, 'and mark my words, Mannerling will soon be up for sale.'

Isabella surveyed her father, suddenly exhausted, wondering whether he had gone mad.

'That will not help us,' said Isabella. 'How could we ever afford to buy it back?'

Sir William rubbed his hands together nervously. 'Lord Fitzpatrick appeared much taken with you, Isabella.'

Isabella flushed. 'What has that to do with anything?'

'I learned tonight that despite his being Irish, he is immensely wealthy. Were he to marry you, you could suggest he sells that pawky house and estate, what's-its-name, Perival, and buy Mannerling instead.'

Isabella took a deep breath. Barry hovered over the tea-things, frightened to make a noise and draw attention to himself.

'I did not tell you, Papa, but Lord Fitzpatrick proposed marriage to me last week and I turned him down and blurted out that Mr Judd was to announce his engagement to me at the ball. He was naturally furious with me and his aunt is disgusted with all of us. So thanks to the madness of the Beverley pride, we have lost two good friends. I do not think I want tea. Pray excuse me.'

She walked from the room, leaving a stunned silence behind her. Then Sir William saw Barry and found his voice. 'Hey, you, fellow, leave that and get out of here.'

Barry left. The front door was standing open. He looked out. Isabella was walking across the lawn, her muslin gown floating about her slim body.

He ran after her. 'Beg pardon, miss, but will you be long? I want to know when to lock up for the night.'

She turned to face him. 'I need some time by myself,' she said quietly. 'I will lock up when I return.'

He turned to go. 'Stay,' said Isabella suddenly. 'If I do not talk to someone sensible, then I will go mad.'

There was a fallen log at the end of the lawn. She made to sit on it, but Barry said, 'You will ruin your gown.' He took off his jacket and spread it on the log.

Isabella sat down. 'Join me,' she said, and Barry sat down next to her.

The air was warm and the night was quiet and still. At last Isabella said, 'It seems I am a failure.'

'Now to my reckoning, you be a success,' said Barry. 'Miss, I was praying and praying that you would not marry Mr Judd. Look at the manner of man you have observed this night!'

'I know, I know,' said Isabella wretchedly. 'Now what am I to do?'

His voice sounded out, flat and even in the quiet night. 'Forget Mannerling.'

'I cannot,' whispered Isabella.

'May I make a suggestion, miss, if I may be so bold? I fear that the reason the Beverley family will not let go of Mannerling is because they might have to accept and live with their present circumstances.'

Isabella turned and looked at him haughtily. She was sharply aware that she, Isabella Beverley, was conversing on intimate terms with a mere servant, and only an odd man at that. But the angry retort which rose to her lips suddenly died away. The full import of what he had just said sank in and she knew it to be true.

Instead she said, 'Perhaps now I can begin to accept our new circumstances. But the others cannot . . . will not. They looked to me to save them.'

'Then you must look now to yourself, miss. 'Tis a pity about Lord Fitzpatrick. There's a real gentleman.'

But Isabella was too ashamed to think about Lord Fitzpatrick or his aunt. She had used both of them ruthlessly. She had not even learned how to flirt, but she had been beginning to learn friendship but not the value of it.

She rose. 'I must go in or they will come looking for me. I can only hope Jessica is asleep because I could not bear any more recriminations tonight.'

But Jessica was awake and waiting in the bedroom, her eyes hot and angry. 'Now what are we to do?' she burst out. 'It is too bad of you, Isabella. You could have managed Judd.'

'I have no wish to manage, as you put it, such a creature as Mr Judd,' said Isabella. 'Mary and he are well suited.'

'But such a lowly creature as Mary to be mistress of Mannerling and all its treasures!'

'After tonight's exhibition,' said Isabella, stretching her hands behind her back and beginning to unfasten the tapes of her ballgown, 'I doubt if there will soon be many treasures left. We must give up any idea of Mannerling, Jessica, and accept our circumstances.'

'Give up Mannerling!' Jessica strode up and down the small bedroom, clenching and unclenching her hands. 'And to think I used to look up to you, Isabella. You have changed. You even talk familiarly to the servants. You have forgot who you are.'

'My sole wish,' said Isabella, taking off her gown and throwing it over a chair, 'is to forget the type of person I was. I am weary and I cannot bear you giving me a jaw-me-dead, Jessica. If you think Judd is such a prize, get him yourself!'

'And how easy will that be now he is engaged to Mary? It should have been left to me. I would not have failed.'

Isabella went over to the toilet-table and filled a basin with water. 'What do you know of men, Jessica? You are the way I was until recently. You only think of them as commodities, as bearers of land and houses and money.'

'Any minute now you are going to talk about true love,' jeered Jessica.

'If you are going to go on and on, I am going to change places with Lizzie and you can complain to her,' threatened Isabella.

'As if that would do any good.' Jessica's face was hard with contempt. 'We all think you have failed us.'

Are they all mad? wondered Isabella when Jessica had finally fallen asleep. This so-called pride of the Beverleys is a sham. How can they feel other than grateful that I had such a lucky escape?

She fell into an uneasy sleep and dreamt she was running towards the temple, crying out, 'No! No!' and then seeing the whole edifice disintegrate in front of her eyes.

It was soon to be borne in on the hitherto neglected Beverleys that Mr Judd's behaviour at his ball had restored them to society. Lady Tarrant was the first to call, and after her, in the succeeding days, came carriage after carriage and invitation after invitation to balls and routs and parties. But neither Mrs Kennedy nor the viscount called.

A month later, the Beverleys once more set out for a ball, at Lady Tarrant's this time. They were all mentally geared up to facing the sight of Mr Judd and Mary Stoppard. But when they arrived, there was no sign of either. Lady Beverley said in what she hoped was a casual manner, 'I suppose we shall be meeting the terrible Mr Judd.'

'Good gracious, no,' said Lady Tarrant roundly. 'No one is going to ask *them* anywhere ever again. Such disgraceful behaviour!' Lady Tarrant had already voiced her horror at Mr Judd's behaviour, but the Beverleys, even Isabella, had naively thought that the owner of such a pearl as Mannerling must be forgiven everything. Yet it became apparent to her, as the ball progressed, that Mr Judd was being generally snubbed and not invited anywhere, and she took comfort from the thought that the scheming and devious Mary as well as Mr Judd was being socially ostracized.

And then she forget about them for the viscount entered the ballroom, with Mrs Kennedy on his arm. He looked as handsome and carefree as ever. Had he avoided looking at her, Isabella might have comforted herself with the thought that he still felt something for her, but he stopped beside her, bowed and smiled very pleasantly, and then moved on. That she should wish he still retained some feeling for her came as a surprise and, usually an excellent dancer, she stumbled several times in the steps of the

127

cotillion and in the following waltz actually trod on her partner's toes.

She began to hope that the viscount might relent, that he might take her up for the supper dance, but he bowed before a pretty little debutante, a Miss Jardey, and then led her into supper. Isabella herself was escorted by a young army captain called Charles Farmer. He was fresh-faced and had a jolly laugh and talked about how much he was looking forward to the start of the hunting season while Isabella was all too aware that the viscount was sitting along from her at the table, a few places away. She could hear his laugh. Miss Jardey appeared to be keeping him well amused. He would probably marry someone like Miss Jardey who would appreciate him, who would have Mrs Kennedy as a friend, and Miss Jardey would ride Satan. All that she had nearly had and now had lost hit her like a blow. She tried to think of Mannerling, but all she could do was marvel at her obsession for her old home, an obsession which had now left her.

'Do you hunt?' she realized the captain was asking her.

'No, I do not,' said Isabella. 'And now, as we have no horses, I could not, even if I wanted to.'

'As to that,' he said awkwardly, 'I would be honoured . . . consider it a privilege . . . to supply you with a mount.'

Isabella smiled at him. 'That is very kind of you, sir, but I have no interest in hunting. Dear me, how rude I sound! I am interested in your stories of hunting, of course I am. I simply meant I have no interest in taking part in the sport.'

The captain lowered his voice. 'It's a shame what happened to your family. No horses! I tell you what, I'll bring a carriage over, provided your parents give you permission, and take you and your sisters out for a drive. There's an interesting ruin . . . Dear me, my wicked tongue. The last thing you probably want to see is a ruin.'

'So long as it isn't on the grounds of Mannerling, I should be delighted,' said Isabella.

'I say, I shall be the envy of all having such a bevy of beauties in my carriage,' said the captain. 'Mama has a barouche I could borrow which would be just the thing.'

'Where is this ruin, and what is it a ruin of?' asked Isabella.

'It's a Norman tower a few miles from Hedgefield. It's all that's left of a castle. It is covered in ivy. Most romantic. And it commands a splendid view.'

'If you drive us,' suggested Isabella, 'we could bring a picnic.'

'Capital.' His face fell. He wondered suddenly just how impoverished the Beverleys were and whether it would be rude to suggest he bring a picnic hamper himself. Almost as if she had read his thoughts, she said gently, 'We are blessed with an excellent cook.'

His face cleared. 'Oh, in that case . . . Would tomorrow be too soon?'

'Perhaps the day after,' suggested Isabella. 'I cannot see my parents making any objection.' Surely they would not start questioning the captain's lineage and fortune.

'I haven't been to Mr Stoppard's church since the Mannerling ball,' said Isabella. 'Do you go yourself?'

'Yes, I and my family still go. But you do not?'

'We go to the church in Hedgefield.'

'Not walking, surely!'

'Not as bad as that. Papa hires a carriage, or sometimes the squire, Sir Jeffrey Blane, comes to collect us all.'

The captain blushed. 'Forgive me. I should not be discussing your . . . er . . . new circumstances in this way.'

'Indeed, Captain Farmer, it is a relief to talk openly. We have never asked for help before or taken favours and now we must, and I think it might be good for us,' said Isabella, resolutely forgetting how her parents took every kindness as their due and even ordered the squire's coachman on Sundays as if he were their own.

Captain Charles Farmer began to feel very much at ease and older than his twenty years, very much a man of the world. Here he was sitting beside the most dazzling beauty in the county and chatting away on intimate terms. And she was to go driving with him, along with all her gorgeous sisters. He prayed fervently that the day would be fine so all could observe his triumph.

He began to tell her of his military adventures and Isabella became quite absorbed in his tales, although she did privately remark that he seemed to be the hero of every one and wondered where truth stopped and embellishment began.

Then he stopped in mid-sentence and looked alarmed. 'I must be boring you dreadfully, Miss Isabella. Ladies are not expected to listen to military matters.'

'Fustian. I am quite fascinated, sir.'

'Really?' The captain looked at her with such a comical mixture of gratification and surprise that Isabella laughed.

The viscount heard that laugh and his face darkened. How dare she enjoy herself?

He had imagined an Isabella isolated from society and company by that damned Beverley pride and given plenty of space and time to think of what she had lost, namely his love. He had imagined her standing by the window looking out, hoping to see him ride up. She had no right to look so beautiful or act in that carefree manner. He craned his head forward. Young Farmer, by all that was holy. So the pride of the Beverleys had finally broken and haughty Miss Isabella was setting her cap at a mere pup when she could have had him!

'You wook so fierce,' said Miss Jardey with a nervous laugh. 'Ickle me is all a-twemble.'

The viscount's blue eyes fastened on her. 'Were you born with a speech defect, or are you merely following the irritating fashion of speaking like a baby?'

'Weally!' declared Miss Jardey, turning her head away and beginning to prattle to the gentleman on her other side.

The viscount drank his wine and brooded until the end of the supper. He found himself tailing Isabella and the captain back to the ballroom. He followed at a discreet distance, saw Isabella and the captain approach the Beverley parents. He saw the captain say something, saw Lady Beverley's initial haughty look of surprise and thought, aha, the captain wishes to take Isabella driving and is about to be refused. But Isabella said something sharply, Sir William murmured a few words and Lady Beverley nodded her head. The viscount pressed closer, in time to hear the captain say cheerfully, 'Good, that's settled. I shall call for you at eleven in the morning the day after tomorrow.' He turned to Isabella. 'You will like the Norman ruin. It is said to be haunted.'

Isabella laughed, that charming laugh. 'I do not believe in ghosts or Gothic tales.'

The viscount withdrew quickly before his interest could be observed.

So you do not believe in ghosts, he thought savagely. But you will!

SEVEN

From ghoulies and ghosties and long-leggedy beasties
And things that go bump in the night,
Good Lord, deliver us!

ANONYMOUS

Isabella, for the very first time, felt excluded from her sisters' company. When she joined them in the drawing room, parlour, or garden, they always broke off what they were saying and relapsed into innocuous chit-chat. She knew she was being left out of whatever plans the Beverleys had now of reclaiming Mannerling.

But there was the outing with Captain Farmer to look forward to. The day was not sunny but one of those sort of uniform grey days which happen so frequently in England. The air was very still and damp, but there seemed to be no sign of actual rain.

Captain Farmer arrived driving a large barouche himself. The sisters got in and Joshua loaded a large picnic hamper into the rumble and off they went, Isabella perched on the box beside the captain. They drove through Hedgefield, Captain Farmer nodding to right and left to various friends and acquaintances, feeling very proud to be driving so many beauties.

Isabella, who had been relaxing in his company, felt her pleasant feelings ebbing away as they passed the Green Man. There it had been where she had spent such a happy time with the viscount. Such a man would soon be married.

As if reading her thoughts, the captain said, 'I saw Fitzpatrick when I was out riding yesterday. Charming fellow. Now someone like that should have taken over Mannerling. My sister, Susan, is wild about him, but then so are all the other ladies. How can I compete with a title, good looks, and wealth?' he asked, shooting Isabella a teasing look.

You can't, thought Isabella sadly, but she said aloud, 'You have an engaging manner, Captain, and you are very enjoyable company.'

He flushed with gratification and began to whistle. His father had warned him that he was not to become seriously involved with any of the Beverley sisters. It was his duty to marry some female with a sensible dowry. But he had the knack of living for the moment and therefore was content to be seen driving 'the prettiest woman in England,' which was what he privately thought Isabella to be.

They arrived at the tower, which was perched on a bluff commanding a fine view of the rolling countryside. They could see the silver gleam on the river Severn below them. The tower was covered in ivy.

'Is it possible to climb up it?' asked Lizzie.

'Oh, yes,' said the captain. 'I thought we would all do that after we have our picnic.'

His groom took the basket from the carriage, spread a cloth on the grass, and began to lay everything out. The girls in their pretty gowns sank down on rugs and cushions, which the groom had then provided. As the captain entertained Isabella and poured her wine, Isabella noticed the others were clustered close to Jessica, talking in whispers. She caught the name Fitzpatrick and frowned, causing the alarmed captain to ask if he had said something to offend her.

'Not at all,' said Isabella truthfully, for she had not been listening to a word he had said. She was suddenly sure that Jessica was the one chosen to try to engage the affections of the viscount and then persuade him to buy back Mannerling.

She gave a little shiver. How mercenary they all were! And yet Jessica, with her auburn hair, vitality, and determination might find it easy to capture the viscount. Isabella experienced a stab of jealousy but did not recognize it for what it was, only wondering why she had a sudden intense feeling of dislike for Jessica.

Above their heads, the 'ghost' in the tower waited patiently. He crossed to one of the narrow arrow-slits and looked down. Jessica came into view below him and with her were the twins, Rachel and Abigail. Jessica's clear voice rose up to his listening ears. 'We cannot rely on Isabella any more. It is up to me.'

Rachel said, 'Cannot you woo Mr Judd away from Mary?'

'I do not think so. That one would sue him for

135

breach of promise. No, no, Fitzpatrick is the answer. He will buy Mannerling for us.'

'But,' protested Abigail, 'we have disaffected poor Mrs Kennedy.'

'That was Isabella's doing, not ours. We will call on her tomorrow and I will begin my plan of campaign.'

They moved off. The 'ghost,' Lord Fitzpatrick himself, moved away from the window. He was now anxious for them to inspect the tower. He was going to give them the fright of their lives.

Down below, among the remains of the picnic, Isabella and the captain had been joined by the others. Isabella was laughing and protesting there were no such things as ghosts, but the captain said quite seriously, 'It is said that the ghost of a Norman knight haunts this tower.'

Isabella's sisters began to look nervous. The day was growing darker. 'I think it is going to rain,' said little Lizzie uneasily. 'Perhaps we should come another day when . . . when it is sunny.'

The captain signalled to his groom. 'Hitch up the horses again. We will just climb up and have a look and then we will return home. You cannot leave without a look.'

Chattering and giggling, the girls entered the tower, Jessica in the lead and Isabella and the captain following in the rear.

The old stone stairs were broken in places. The wind had risen and moaned about the old tower, setting the ivy rustling, casting odd flickering shadows through the arrow-slits.

The giggles died away, a silence fell on the party.

'Nearly there,' called back Jessica. The steps led straight into a small circular room at the top.

She stood on the threshold and then stopped short, her hand to her mouth.

The disembodied head of a Norman knight in helmet and vizor appeared to float in the gloom. His eyes were glittering and he was surrounded by an eerie greenish light.

Lizzie peered round Jessica and began to scream. Isabella found her sisters crushing past her in their panic to escape.

'What on earth . . . ?' began the captain. Then, 'Wait there,' he said to Isabella.

He stared into the room. The 'ghost' stared back. And then a voice from the grave whispered, 'Begone!'

The captain turned as white as paper. He thrust blindly past Isabella and hurtled down the stairs. The other sisters were already huddled in the carriage, clutching each other. The captain sprang to the box, shouted to the horses, and the carriage hurtled crazily off. It was only when they had gone some miles and were nearly at Hedgefield that the terrified captain realized he had left Isabella behind.

Isabella stood outside the top room, petrified, too scared to move. Dimly she heard the carriage driving off and then there was only the sound of the wind. She began to edge slowly backwards down the stairs. Nothing was going to make her look in that tower room.

And then a great voice cried, '*Wooooo!*'

She turned and ran, stumbling down the broken stairs, and once outside the tower, ran desperately in the direction of the road.

In the tower room, the viscount tore down the curtain of green gauze which he had hung before his face, blew out the oil-lamp with its green-stained glass, took off the helmet and threw it in the corner of the room. He opened the lapels of his black coat, which he had closed to cover the whiteness of his shirt, darted lightly down the stairs and ran to a stand of trees where he had concealed his horse. He set off across the fields, which would bring him onto the road ahead of the fleeing Isabella, urged his mount over the last fence, and once on the road, slowed to an easy canter, looking for all the world like any English gentleman out for a sedate ride.

The whole 'haunting' had gone better than he had expected.

But he felt a sharp pang of conscience as he saw, down the length of the road, Isabella running towards him, hatless, her hair tumbling about her shoulders, her face white.

He reined in beside her and swung himself down from the saddle. Isabella gave a gasp and threw herself into his arms. Soft curls tickled his nose, firm breasts were pressed against his chest, and he experienced a swimming feeling of sweetness.

'There's a ghost . . . a ghost,' she babbled. 'Back there . . . in the tower.'

'There, now,' he said, hugging her. 'It must have been a trick of the light and the moving ivy.'

She disengaged herself, blushing, and making a great effort, she said, 'Are you sure? But the others saw something, and Captain Farmer was so frightened out of his wits that he ran off and left me.'

'Dear me, your swains do seem to have a habit of abandoning you to your fate, do they not? You had best let me escort you home.'

Isabella hesitated. 'What is the matter?' he asked.

'I do . . . did not believe in ghosts, and you see, I did not look in the top room of the tower, which is where the others saw something. Do you believe in ghosts?'

'No,' said the viscount firmly and then immediately regretted his denial, for Isabella put up her chin and declared, 'Please accompany me back to the tower, my lord. I would see for myself. I thought I heard a wail, but that could have been the wind.'

He glanced up at the sky. 'It looks like rain and you have already had a bad fright and you have lost your hat.'

'It does not matter. Do you not see? I must find out. I am the eldest. If it turns out to be a mere trick of the light, then I can tell my sisters that. Poor little Lizzie will have nightmares.'

'Very well,' he said reluctantly.

He mounted his horse, and leaning down, pulled her up to sit in front of him, and with one firm arm around her waist he rode off in the direction of the tower.

Isabella was surprised to find it was so close. She felt she had run away from it for miles and miles.

As he helped her down, she felt a spasm of sheer

terror and clutched at his arm. 'Would you like to wait here?' asked the viscount.

But Isabella resolutely shook her head. 'No, I must be brave. Lead on!'

The viscount mounted the stairs. He wondered if he could reach the room well before her so that he could try to hide the evidence of the haunting in some dark corner, but she pressed close behind him, not wanting to be left on her own.

The game is up, thought the viscount, but at least she will not guess I was the prankster.

He strode confidently into the tower room. 'Look,' he said to Isabella, 'here is your ghost.' He picked up the helmet in one hand and the green gauze in the other.

Isabella stared at them. 'So someone hid here to frighten us to death. What a monster! Who knew of our outing?'

'Young Farmer has many friends, army friends, young and heedless.'

'Monstrous! But at least I can put my sisters' fears to rest.'

'Then I had better get you home quickly. Captain Farmer will have a search party looking for you by now.'

Isabella began to laugh with relief. 'How frightened I was. And I lost one of my best bonnets in my flight.'

She turned and went down the stairs and he followed her. But as Isabella was about to leave the tower, she drew back with an exclamation of dismay. The rain had started to fall, steady, drumming rain.

The viscount looked over her shoulder. 'We cannot

leave in this downpour. Come, sit over here.' He pointed to a flat slab of masonry. 'I will go and find some shelter under the trees for my horse.' He took off his coat and put it about her shoulders and then ran off into the rain.

When he returned, his fine cambric shirt was wet and raindrops glistened in his thick hair. He sat down beside Isabella, thinking she had never looked more beautiful than she did at that moment, with her hair tumbled about her shoulders.

'So tell me,' he asked, 'what led you to believe that Mr Judd was going to announce his engagement to *you* at the ball?'

Isabella hung her head. 'He courted me. He sent me presents. He . . . kissed me.'

'The devil he did! So the whole idea was to humiliate you and your family. Why?'

'Betty, one of the maids, said that the night you brought me back after rescuing me from the field, she saw Mr Judd listening at the parlour window. That was when we were talking about my marrying Mr Judd to get Mannerling back.'

He thought of the conversation he had recently overheard and gave a wry smile. 'You and your sisters should be more careful when you are plotting. Anyone could be listening. You should also be more careful with your kisses.'

Isabella blushed and her eyes filled with tears. She was conscious of his nearness, of the warmth emanating from his body, of his wet shirt clinging to his powerful chest.

'Don't cry,' he said softly. He tilted her chin up and kissed her gently on the lips, and then harder, feeling a tremendous surge of passion.

Isabella buried her small white hands in his hair and returned his kiss, deaf and blind to everything but the feel of warm strong lips bearing down on her own.

And then he suddenly drew back and said, 'Listen! What's that?'

From outside came cries and shouts.

He smiled at her tenderly. 'The search party, or I am much mistaken.'

They walked to the doorway and looked out.

A strange sight met their eyes. Men carrying torches were coming across the field towards the tower, fanning out. In the vanguard was the squire, pushing in front of him a trembling Mr Stoppard, who was holding up a large cross.

The viscount laughed. 'They probably think you have been dragged off to hell.' He waved and pointed to Isabella standing next to him.

The look of relief on Mr Stoppard's face was comical. The viscount shrewdly guessed his relief was not so much at the sight of Isabella safe and well but the realization that he did not have to face any phantom.

Sir Jeffrey Blane, the squire, came hurrying up. Behind him, Isabella saw her father approaching.

'My dear child,' cried the squire, 'what on earth has been happening? That young fool, Farmer, told us some tale of a frightful ghost and how he had run off with the others and left you.'

'Someone was playing tricks,' said Isabella. 'You

142

will find, up in the tower room, a Norman helmet and some green gauze and a lantern. That is your ghost.'

Sir William had now joined them. His eyes darted from his daughter's flushed and happy face to that of the viscount.

'Do I take it, Lord Fitzpatrick,' he said, 'that you have been *alone* in this tower with my daughter?'

'We had to shelter from the rain,' said the viscount quietly. He drew a little away from Isabella, as if he knew what Sir William was about to say next.

'Well, my dear Fitzpatrick,' said Sir William, rubbing his hands gleefully, 'it appears you will have to make an honest woman of my daughter.'

'Don't be a fool!' snapped the viscount. 'When did sheltering from the rain with a gentleman count as compromising a lady's honour?'

'Yes, indeed,' said the squire in amazement. 'In faith, sir, you should be thanking Fitzpatrick here for having minded your daughter instead of trying to force him to marry the girl.'

Others had clustered about and were listening eagerly.

Isabella wondered whether it was possible to die on the spot from shame.

The viscount's face was hard with contempt.

'But,' said Sir William with awful eagerness, 'you are dishevelled, Isabella, and where is your bonnet?'

Goodbye, love, thought Isabella bleakly. Aloud, she said, 'I will tell you what happened. Captain Farmer and my sisters in their great fright ran off and left me. I was at first too frightened to move and then

143

the prankster in the tower let out a wail and I fled. In my flight my hair came down and I lost my bonnet. When I gained the road, I found Lord Fitzpatrick riding towards me. He suggested, as it was about to rain and that you would be worried, that he should take me straight home. But I had recovered my wits and remembered that I do not believe in ghosts and so I persuaded my lord to accompany me to the tower. We found the evidence that it had all been a trick and were prepared to leave, and then the downpour started. We had only been waiting at the entrance to the tower a few moments when you arrived. And now, Papa, if you consider you have shamed me enough, may I please go home.'

The viscount looked at her dejected face. He wanted to cry out that he would marry her, but, firstly, to do so would mean that the listeners would think something had happened between them that made him think he ought to. Then, secondly, he could only remember his own passion. A horrible thought that Isabella might be party to the Beverleys's plan to get him to marry one of them and then try to get him to buy Mannerling would not leave his mind. And so he said nothing as Isabella was led away towards the road, towards the waiting carriages.

Mr Ajax Judd wandered gloomily through the stately rooms of Mannerling. Faintly, from across the lawns, filtered the sounds of the workmen repairing the temple. With all the superstitious nature of the true gambler, Mr Judd felt the falling of his fortunes was due to the blowing up of the temple. Now he was tied to a woman he did not really rate very highly and had only used to irritate the Beverleys. But Mary had made great friends with his mother and to get rid of her appeared unthinkable. He had not realized just how much money was entailed in running an estate like Mannerling. Certainly it was in good heart, but he had invested money on various ventures on the Stock Exchange thinking that they might prosper, only to lose money. He had paid a brief visit to London to gamble in St James's, with disastrous results.

He felt Mannerling was punishing him. It was almost as if the great house had a soul, had thoughts. He loved it all with a passion. In an effort to placate it as he would have tried to placate a human being, he had rehung the Beverley ancestors in the Long Gallery, had bought back some of the paintings he had sold and put them back in place. The heavy Jacobean furniture, which he liked so much but Mannerling did not seem to, had been consigned to the bonfire and the pretty, light drawing room pieces restored to their former places.

He paused on the landing and patted the banister. 'There now,' he whispered. 'Everything will be as it was. Change my luck for me. I must keep you.'

Isabella faced her family in the drawing room. Sir William stood with his back to her, staring at the window. In a clipped cold voice, Isabella told them what had happened and about how her father had tried to constrain Lord Fitzpatrick to marry her.

145

'And,' said Isabella, glaring at Jessica, 'I know you are probably plotting to see if you can get Lord Fitzpatrick for yourself. Well, mark my words, after this day, he will certainly have nothing to do with this family ever again.'

'We must think of something,' said Lady Beverley. 'Perhaps a present for Mrs Kennedy . . . ?'

Her voice trailed away before the wrath in her eldest daughter's eyes.

'Cannot you understand?' shouted Isabella. 'MAN-NERLING IS GONE!'

She turned on her heel and left the room. She went up to the bedchamber she shared with Jessica and flung herself face down on the bed.

She heard Jessica come in but did not look up. 'I shall not give up so easily,' she heard Jessica say fiercely. 'I am going to Perival tomorrow to make my peace with Mrs Kennedy and see what I can do.'

'Go away,' said Isabella in a muffled voice. 'You weary me.'

The weather was dry and breezy as Jessica and the twins set out for Perival. Isabella, watching them go from an upstairs window, noticed that a gig and a horse had been hired for them, so Sir William knew why they were going. A man had been hired from Hedgefield to drive them. Isabella thought they would have been better to take Barry. He would at least comfort them after they had been snubbed. But then Jessica would never turn to a mere servant for comfort.

Jessica was in high spirits. She was taking *action*,

not like that widgeon, Isabella, who had now let two men slip through her fingers. Rachel and Abigail were infected by her high spirits. Barry had been right in what he had said to Isabella. The Beverleys were determined to live in hope, for to accept the fact they had lost Mannerling forever would be to accept their changed circumstances.

As they were approaching Mannerling, for the road to Perival took them past the gates, Mary Stoppard could be seen in an open carriage with her father coming down the drive of Mannerling. The lodge-keeper ran to open the gates for them.

Mary saw Jessica and the twins. Her black eyes flashed with triumph as they raked over the shabby hired gig and then she gave them a brief little nod before her father drove her right past them.

'Did you see that?' demanded Jessica furiously. 'Giving herself all the airs of the lady she is not! Well, let's see her face when Mannerling is bought back by us!'

The old horse which was pulling the gig clopped lazily along the winding country road which led to Perival. 'I'm hungry,' said Rachel.

'Never mind,' consoled Jessica. 'Mrs Kennedy will be so glad to see us that she will provide us with tea or even a cold collation.' For Mrs Kennedy's dislike could only be temporary. A visit from any of the Beverleys was an honour.

As they drove up the drive to Perival, Jessica looked all around. There were men putting in full-sized trees and men gardening. She gave a little smile. Lord

Fitzpatrick was obviously as rich as her father had heard him to be.

She could see that the windows of the drawing room upstairs were open and she could see the comfortable figure of Mrs Kennedy. And then the viscount came into view and bent over his aunt and said something.

'Both at home,' said Jessica with satisfaction, for she had begun to think that she should have sent Barry over with a letter first, which was what she originally had planned to do.

She waited impatiently for the driver to jump down and knock at the door, but he was only a hired driver and so he just sat there.

She climbed down herself and performed a brisk tattoo on the brass knocker.

There was a silence and then the door opened and the butler stood there.

Jessica handed him her card and asked for both Mrs Kennedy and Lord Fitzpatrick.

'Wait there, miss,' he said. He took the card and she could see him mounting the stairs.

She was just turning to tell the twins to get down from the gig, so sure was she of her welcome, when she heard the butler returning.

He bowed slightly and said, 'Neither Mrs Kennedy nor my lord are at home.'

Jessica blushed painfully. The cut direct!

She turned and walked to the gig, as stiff as an outraged cat.

'Take us home,' she said to the driver.

'What happened?' asked Abigail.

Jessica frowned her to silence. A hired driver must not know of the Beverleys's humiliation.

How long and weary the journey back seemed!

'They are here and so soon!' cried Sir William, who had been standing at the drawing room window.

Isabella slipped quietly through to the kitchen, smiled wanly at Joshua, and then escaped into the back garden. She saw the comforting figure of Barry over by the hen-run and went to join him.

'Trouble, miss?' he asked.

The hens scratched and uttered sounds like rusty gates.

'I think so,' said Isabella. 'I did not wait to hear the news. But when my sister Jessica and the twins go calling on Lord Fitzpatrick and return very quickly, looking miserable, I can only assume they were snubbed. So this is it, is it, Barry? Brookfield House for ever and ever, amen?'

'And not a bad place either, if I may say so, miss,' said Barry. 'And if I may also say so, cards are still arriving. You will have plenty of amusements. You go to the squire's garden fête on Saturday, do you not?'

'I believe so. Yes, yes, of course. The good squire is sending the carriage for us. At least Captain Farmer will be there,' added Isabella, half to herself.

Barry threw the last of the grain to the hens and put down the bowl. 'As to that, miss, I did hear on good authority that the young captain was so thoroughly ashamed of himself and his cowardly behaviour in running off and leaving you that he has rejoined his regiment.'

'And who exactly is this good authority?'

'Sir William, miss. He received a letter from the captain this morning. You know, miss, thinking about military men and all that, the squire's son, Harry, now, he is expected to be at the fête and he is an army captain. Have you met him?'

'No, but I have heard of him.'

'He is accounted handsome, miss, and very genial.'

'I do believe you are trying to matchmake for me, Barry,' said Isabella with a smile as she thought how the old Isabella would shun the mere suggestion that she should be at all interested in a mere squire's son. But then the old Isabella would not have stooped to converse on friendly terms with any servant.

'Heaven forbid,' said Barry. 'It is only that it is pleasant for a young lady to meet a friendly and easy-going gentleman.'

Isabella looked around her. 'So this is it, finally,' she said. 'This is home.'

'Until you get married, miss.'

Isabella began to walk away. She said over her shoulder, 'That day may never come.'

She went indoors, hearing the murmur of voices from the drawing room. She went upstairs and changed into a walking dress and half-boots, went out again and began to make her way across the fields.

She thought of what she had so nearly had and what she had thrown away. Lord Fitzpatrick's face rose before her eyes. He would marry soon and would probably be happy and consider himself well quit of the Beverley family. Mary would make sure all the

Beverleys were invited to her wedding to witness her 'triumph.'

But Mary was to be pitied, not envied. Isabella wondered whether the queer spell that Mannerling cast on everyone had infected Mary or whether she just saw it as a grand house of which she would soon be the mistress. Her thoughts turned back to the viscount. He would be at the squire's fete. It would be painful to attend, for everyone would know about how her father had tried to coerce the viscount into marrying her.

She toyed with the idea of pretending to be ill. But then that would mean staying at home and wondering whom the viscount was speaking to, whom he was flirting with. All she could do was put on a brave face and ignore the looks and whispers.

On the day of the fête, Isabella took some comfort from the fact that Jessica's humiliation had seemed to put an end to her father's mad schemes, although Sir William was already the worse for drink when they set out in the carriage the squire had sent for them.

Lizzie, sitting quietly in a corner of the carriage, reflected that they all looked very fine in their India muslins. But gowns did not last forever and Lizzie, as the youngest, knew the day would soon come when she had to be content with her sisters' hand-me-downs. She felt she could be content at Brookfield if only Mrs Kennedy would come back again and fill the house with activity and bustle and things to do.

They could hear the noise of a band playing a jolly tune as they approached the squire's. Tables had been set out on the lawns and there was a marquee where the dancing would take place later.

The squire and his wife met them and proudly introduced their son, Harry.

He was an engaging-looking young man with curly fair hair worn longer than the current fashion. He had grey eyes which danced with laughter. His face was lightly tanned and he had a good figure, although he was quite small in stature.

Those grey eyes fastened appreciatively on the elegant picture Isabella made in a white muslin gown with a wide green sash and broad-brimmed straw hat embellished with silk flowers.

'Father,' he said, turning to the squire, 'the guests are almost all arrived. I shall escort Miss Isabella.'

The squire, Sir Jeffrey Blane, felt he could hardly protest and comforted himself with the thought that Harry was soon to rejoin his regiment. In any case, the boy had already been told not to become romantically involved with the Beverleys, for the girls could not command any reasonable sort of dowries.

'We are lucky with the weather, are we not?' said Harry Blane, leading Isabella across the lawn. 'A perfect summer's day. I was lucky to get leave in order to be here.'

'Will the war never end?' asked Isabella, referring to the battles raging in the Peninsula.

'Oh, we will win in the end, never fear. It is a delight to talk to you, Miss Isabella. We have been neighbours for so long and yet we have never met before.'

Isabella reflected that they had never been on

intimate terms with the Blanes before, the Beverleys considering a mere squire and his family not important enough.

Mary Stoppard came up on the arm of Mr Judd. Mr Judd hailed Isabella. 'The temple's being repaired,' he said eagerly.

Isabella looked at him in surprise. 'Surely it was silly to blow the thing up, only to have to restore it?'

He appeared not to hear her. 'And I have rehung your ancestors in the Long Gallery,' he went on, still with that strange eagerness in his voice.

Isabella tugged at Harry's arm as a signal she wanted to move on. She gave a little bow.

'Was that the famous Mr Judd of Mannerling?' asked Harry when they were out of earshot.

'Yes, and how rude of me not to introduce you. I thought you knew him. With him was his intended bride, the vicar's daughter, Mary Stoppard.'

'Oh, I know *her*. So her father has toad-eaten his daughter into a good marriage at last. I wish her the joy of him. Judd seems quite mad.'

'He certainly behaved very oddly. At the Mannerling ball, you must have heard this, the piece de resistance, apart from the announcement of his forthcoming marriage, was when he blew up the Greek temple. Now it appears he is restoring it. I wonder why. Such a great deal of unnecessary expense.'

'And deuced odd that he should rehang the Beverley ancestors,' exclaimed Harry. 'What's so special about that? They ain't his ancestors.'

It must be Mannerling, thought Isabella suddenly,

Mannerling casting its weird spell on Mr Judd, Mannerling demanding that all should be as it was. She had said she did not believe in ghosts but she began to wonder if Mannerling was a haunted house, a strange place which demanded absolute love from its owners.

And then she forgot about Mannerling, for the viscount had arrived. Mrs Kennedy was not with him. Isabella hoped the old lady was well. It was unlike her to miss any event. Isabella began to chatter to Harry in an animated way, all the time conscious of the tall presence across the garden.

When they went to take their seats at the table, she found to her dismay that not only was she seated well away from the viscount, but in such a position that she could not see him at all. She felt such a great degree of frustration and then of sadness and loss that she found it hard to maintain a polite conversation with the gentlemen on either side of her.

Her head ached by the end of the meal and she longed to go home, but there was dancing to follow. Her hand for the first dance was promptly claimed by Harry. It was a rowdy country dance and Isabella was pretending with all her might that she was enjoying herself immensely so that the viscount's attention might be distracted from the pretty girl he was dancing with, when she noticed that Lizzie, who was dancing with a young boy, lost her fan, the cord that held it to her wrist snapping. The fan fell to the grass floor of the marquee. Lizzie gave an exclamation and stopped to retrieve it, but at the same time a stocky young man leaped backwards in the figure of the dance and his large foot came down onto the delicate fan, snapping the ivory sticks and crushing it into the grass.

Isabella watched anxiously as Lizzie, her face paper-white, bent to try to retrieve the pieces of the fan. Her partner was laughing and trying to pull her away, but Lizzie suddenly stood up and darted out of the marquee.

'My sister, I must go after her,' said Isabella, and before Harry could stop her, she, too, ran out of the marquee.

She stood outside, looking this way and that. Behind her, the tumty-tumty music of the band sounded on the summer air. Isabella ran to the house and questioned the servants. A little maid said she had seen a young lady running through the gardens at the back of the house towards the river.

'The river!' echoed Isabella with a feeling of dread.

She hurtled through the gardens, down over the lawn, jumped the ha-ha, straight towards the rushing noise of the river, calling, 'Lizzie! Lizzie!' at the top of her voice.

She had just about gained the river bank when a strong arm pulled her round and demanded, 'What is the matter?'

Isabella looked up into the viscount's face and said on a choked sob, 'Lizzie! She is upset. She was seen running for the river.'

He dropped her arm and ran along the river bank, adding his cries of 'Lizzie' to those of Isabella.

And then they saw her, a sad little figure standing

on the edge of a jutting-out flat stone which overhung a deep pool. Her face was pinched and white and her eyes had a blind look.

'Lizzie!' screamed Isabella at the top of her voice.

The little face turned to look first at Isabella and then at the viscount. She gave an odd little wave of her hand and jumped.

'She can't swim,' shouted Isabella.

The viscount tore off his coat and boots and dived into the pool from the other side while Isabella wrung her hands and prayed to God to save her little sister.

The viscount's black head surfaced. He was clutching Lizzie to him as he struck out for the bank. Isabella ran round and, lying on her stomach, she reached down and grabbed Lizzie's arm and pulled her up onto the grassy bank on the opposite side of the pool from where Lizzie had jumped.

Lizzie was coughing and spluttering, having only suffered from having swallowed several mouthfuls of clear river water.

'You bad girl!' shrieked Isabella, shaking her wet sister furiously. 'Why did you do it?'

The viscount climbed out and immediately headed round the pool and climbed up to the flat rock from which Lizzie had jumped. He snapped off a stout branch and began digging feverishly at the soft earth and moss under the rock.

'It was the fan,' snivelled Lizzie.

'The fan?' Isabella, quieter now that her great fright was over, stopped shaking her and hugged her close. 'Your fan was broken. What of it?'

156

'It was my prettiest fan,' whispered Lizzie. 'I will never be able to afford another like it.'

'We still have plenty of pretty fans,' said Isabella. 'You may choose from mine, anything you want.'

'But don't you see,' said Lizzie, 'the fan was a symbol.'

'Of what?'

'Of Mannerling. It was executed especially. It had a painting of Mannerling on it. We have lost all, Isabella, and we will never go home again.'

'Mannerling, Mannerling, I *hate* Mannerling,' shouted Isabella. 'I will never go there again. Never. Listen to me, Lizzie, I thought you were the most sensible of us all. We can have a good life at Brookfield House. Look at all the balls and parties we are invited to. You must put Mannerling out of your mind or the place will drive us mad, and it nearly killed you.'

People were coming running up. 'Oh, what can we tell them?' asked Isabella. 'I cannot say my sister nearly committed suicide over a *house*.'

But the viscount was miraculously taking charge. He was already advancing to meet the crowd.

'All is well,' he said. 'An accident. That stone over there . . .' He pointed to the flat rock which he had managed to dislodge enough to make it look dangerous. 'We were standing admiring the view when it gave way and plunged us all in the pool. Please return to the party. I will take the ladies home. No, no, please go away. The ladies do not want to be seen as they are with their gowns sodden.'

He did not want any sharp-eyed observer to remark

157

that Isabella's gown, except from the parts which had become damp when she was clutching her sister, was quite dry.

He waited until they had gone and then said quietly, 'Come, I will take you home.'

Fortunately, by the time they had returned to the squire's house, everyone, with the exception of Lady Beverley and Isabella's sisters, was back inside the marquee.

'I will take them home,' said the viscount. He turned and ordered a servant to fetch his carriage. 'It was an accident. But as you can see, the ladies are wet.'

'Why do you not put on some dry clothes and return?' said Lady Beverley brightly. 'Mr Blane is asking for you, Isabella.'

Isabella looked at her mother in a sort of wonder but said quietly, 'Perhaps. Pray all of you return to the dance.'

She and the viscount and Lizzie drove home in silence.

When Lizzie had been handed over to the maids and Isabella turned to thank the viscount, he said harshly, 'Have I the right of it? Was your little sister trying to kill herself?'

Isabella nodded. 'It all hit her when her fan broke – that we had lost Mannerling forever – and it temporarily, I hope, turned her brain.'

'So she has excelled you. You would throw away love for a pile of bricks and mortar, but your sister would throw away her life. You are all mad.'

He turned on his heel and strode away. Isabella

stood in the shadowy hall, tears running down her cheeks.

Barry, who had been standing in a corner of the hall, listening, moved quietly away.

Something would have to be done.

EIGHT

Really, if the lower orders don't set us a good example,
what on earth is the use of them?

OSCAR WILDE

Mrs Kennedy listened in amazement as her nephew
told her the tale of Lizzie's attempted suicide.

She raised her hands in horror. 'And to think I
thought that poor lamb was the only sane one out o'
the lot of them! Order the carridge!'

'And just where do you intend to go?' asked the viscount wearily.

'Why, to Brookfield House.'

'That is enough, Aunt Mary. Leave those poxy,
mad, pride-ridden Beverleys alone.'

'That I will not. Sure, that poor little child will be
sick wit' misery and Lady Beverley will hang on to that
lie you told her about the loose rock until Doomsday.
I am going there and I am bringing her back with me
and you cannot stop me.'

'Oh, you are as mad as the rest of them. Go, by
all means, and get snubbed and humiliated for your
pains.'

Mrs Kennedy called servants to bustle about as she had a hamper packed full of all sorts of food, from meat pies to pastries and cakes. With the light of battle in her eyes, she ordered the coachman to drive her to Brookfield House.

Lady Beverley was reclining on a chaise longue in the drawing room when Mrs Kennedy was ushered in. 'To what do we owe the honour of this visit?' asked Lady Beverley languidly, putting one white hand to her brow.

The door opened at that moment and Isabella and her sisters came in, with the exception of Lizzie.

Mrs Kennedy said, 'I am come to take Lizzie back to Perival with me and nurse her back to health.'

Lady Beverley sat up and stared at the Irishwoman in amazement. 'Take Lizzie . . . Why? The dear child fell in the river at the squire's and got a soaking, nothing more. I am . . . ahum . . . perfectly capable of looking after my own children. I am sorry your journey has been wasted.'

Isabella stepped forward. 'I think Lizzie should go,' she said quietly. 'You did not hear the correct story. Lord Fitzpatrick was trying to save our ridiculous pride. When Lizzie's fan broke, it was symbolic to her of all we have lost and she realized for the first time that we would never live in Mannerling again. She did not slip into the river. She jumped. She meant to take her own life. Lord Fitzpatrick loosened the rock on which she had been standing before she jumped so that it would look like an accident. He dived in and saved her life.'

161

'I . . . I cannot bear any more,' whispered Lady Beverley. 'You must be lying, Isabella.'

'No, I am not,' said Isabella. 'Pray come with me, Mrs Kennedy. Your kindness is more than any of us deserve.'

She led the way upstairs to the small dark bedroom where Lizzie lay with her face turned to the wall.

'Now, Lizzie,' said Isabella gently, 'you will rise and get dressed and you will go to Perival with Mrs Kennedy, who is come in person to take you. The change of scene will do your spirits the world of good.' She then went to the doorway and shouted for Betty, the maid, and when the girl came running, ordered her to pack Miss Lizzie's things.

Lizzie rose from bed like a sleep-walker and allowed herself to be dressed.

'I've got a hamper of things delivered to your kitchen,' said Mrs Kennedy robustly, although her shrewd eyes watched Lizzie's still, white face anxiously.

'You are so very kind.' Isabella's voice trembled and Mrs Kennedy looked at her in surprise, for she had put Isabella down in her mind as a scheming, heartless jilt.

With Isabella's arm around her waist, Lizzie was helped down to the carriage. When she was seated beside Mrs Kennedy, Isabella leaned in at the open carriage window and said quietly, 'Thank you from the bottom of my heart, Mrs Kennedy. I apologize humbly to you and your . . . family . . . for my callousness. May I call on Lizzie?'

'Oh, any time you like,' said Mrs Kennedy warmly.

162

'Do not worry about Lizzie. I shall send a man over with daily reports.'

The carriage drove off. Isabella waved her handkerchief and then went indoors to face the recriminations of Lady Beverley, who begged her again and again to say that she had been lying.

By the end of November, Lizzie was still at Perival. She was completely restored to health and spirits but yet dreaded returning home, clinging all the time to Mrs Kennedy and begging to be allowed to stay 'just a little longer.'

The rest of the Beverley family went out to various functions where Isabella sometimes saw the viscount and sometimes she did not, and all the time she remembered how he had kissed her in the tower and tortured herself with the thought that had it not been for her father's pushy vulgarity, the viscount might have asked her to marry him.

And then, at the beginning of December, Mr Judd married Mary Stoppard. The Beverleys did not go to the wedding but learned that it had been a very quiet affair, without any great celebrations.

Barry watched and waited, wondering if there was any way he could bring Isabella and the viscount together. He had gone with Isabella several times when she went to visit Lizzie, but on each occasion the viscount had been absent, probably, thought Barry, due to the fact that on each occasion Isabella had sent a note warning of her coming.

Mrs Kennedy was, however, beginning to warm to

Isabella more on each visit. The girl, she decided, had changed a great deal, and whereas she lacked her earlier spark and animation, there was a quiet humility and gratitude about her which was pleasing. From thinking her nephew had made a lucky escape, she began to wonder if a beautiful and pleasant girl like Isabella, although she probably had little dowry, if any at all, might not be a highly suitable bride for the viscount after all. Mrs Kennedy had long believed that when her nephew married, she would need to move out of the house. But if he married Isabella, she would not need to move at all. They dealt together extremely well.

One dark winter's evening, when a high wind rushed through the newly planted trees about Perival and Lizzie had gone to bed clutching one of the novels which Mrs Kennedy had just had delivered, Mrs Kennedy looked up when her nephew entered the drawing room and put aside her sewing.

'That is one of Isabella Beverley's ball gowns,' he said harshly. 'Will you never be done slaving for that family?'

'Sit down, sit down. There is no need to be driven to a passion by the very sight of the girl's duds. I do not slave for anyone. I am helping Isabella make over a gown for the Christmas ball at Lady Tarrant's.'

'If she had less pride, she would be content to go to balls and parties in gowns which the county have seen before.'

'She is a normal female creature like any other. No lady worth her salt likes to turn up in the same old gown.'

'May I point out that she probably has a wardrobe full of "same old gowns." Mr Judd did not take their vast amount of clothes away.'

'Why is it anything to do with Isabella makes you angry? I declare you are in love with her, and she is in love with you, and you are both being very silly.'

'Hah! If I proposed marriage to that one, the first thing she would demand as a wedding present would be her precious Mannerling.'

'No, she would not. It is my belief she had come to her senses long before Lizzie jumped in the river. But you will never know now, will you? For you are as stubborn as an ox. I was tempted, the last time I received a note from her to say when she would be calling, not to tell you so that you might stay and see for yourself what a sweet girl she has become. She was brought up to be proud and then driven to try to ensnare Judd by what she wrongly thought was her duty to that family. Oh, well, sulk on and see what good it does ye. Why do you not call on the lass to say how-d'ye-do? 'Twould not hurt.'

'I will never call at Brookfield House again,' he said, and strode from the room.

But his aunt's words niggled away in his brain that night, preventing sleep. Could it possibly be that she loved him? He had savagely believed her acceptance of his caresses in the tower was because she was party to her father's plot to coerce him into marriage. But he had kissed her, not she, him! And did she cause the rain to fall at the right moment?

He fell into an uneasy sleep just before dawn,

confident that when he woke up he would once again be buoyed up with all his old resentment of her.

But when he awoke in the morning he was filled with a sudden longing to see her, speak to her, study the expression in her eyes.

He could not bring himself to tell his aunt, however, where he was going. He rode off in the direction of Brookfield House, unaware that his aunt was standing by the upstairs window of the drawing room watching him go, a smile of satisfaction on her face.

Isabella, wrapped in a long fur-lined mantle, was standing talking to Barry by the hen-run when he rode up. He dismounted and walked towards them, leading his horse.

'I'll take that to the stable for you, my lord,' said Barry. Isabella blushed and studied the hens as if she had never seen such interesting birds before.

'No need,' said the viscount. 'I shall not be staying long.'

Barry was torn between a desire to leave the couple alone and yet worried if he did so that they might never get down to what he privately designated as 'business.'

'And how do you go on?' the viscount asked Isabella.

'Very well, I thank you, my lord.'

'The weather is very cold. Perhaps I should not keep you standing here, talking.'

'I suppose not,' said Isabella dismally.

Barry suppressed a click of annoyance. He found his voice. 'Have you observed my fine hen-house, my lord?'

The viscount looked at the shack. 'Very fine,' he said. 'Keep the fox out, does it?'

'Haven't lost a hen yet, my lord,' said Barry proudly. 'I beg you to step inside and have a look.'

'Oh, very well,' said the viscount ungraciously.

'Come as well, Miss Isabella,' urged Barry. 'I am uncommon proud of my work.'

Isabella looked at him and tried hard to mask her irritation. She had already admired the hen-house when he had first built it. The hens were in their run. She followed the viscount into the small shed, which smelled anything but pleasant.

'Excellent,' the viscount was just beginning to say politely when Barry slammed the door on the pair of them, leaving them in semi-darkness.

The viscount tried the door. It was locked fast.

'Is this another of your family's tricks?' he demanded wrathfully. 'Am I supposed to stay in here with you until your loving family consider you have been well and truly compromised?'

'I do not know what is going on,' said Isabella desperately. She raised her voice and shouted, 'Barry, let us out of here immediately.'

'Your little plot won't work,' sneered the viscount, 'for I am about to kick this flimsy edifice to pieces.'

And Isabella slapped him across the face as hard as she could.

He stared down at her in the malodorous gloom of the hen-house, lit only by one small window of glass made from the ends of wine bottles.

Her eyes looked enormous. Her lips were trembling. He cursed softly under his breath and jerked her into his arms and kissed her mouth over and over again, as if trying to quench a thirst, until she moaned softly against his mouth and wound her hands in his thick hair.

'You love me,' he said at last, looking down at her in wonder.

'Yes,' she said simply, 'I think I always will. Please let us get out of here or Papa will indeed turn up and consider it a good opportunity to force you to marry me, and I could not bear that. What sane man would want such in-laws?'

'I am not sane,' he said huskily. 'My senses are reeling. Kiss me!'

And she did, while outside, Barry pressed his ear harder against the wood. Ask her outright to marry you, he prayed silently.

But the couple were too intent on kissing and stroking and murmuring sweet nothings for quite some time. At last the viscount said, 'And you are not going to ask me to buy Mannerling for you should it come up for sale?'

'I never want to see the place again,' said Isabella.

'We are going to be married, are we not?'

Isabella leaned her head against his chest and sighed, 'Oh, yes, my darling, my heart, I would like that above all things.'

He crushed her lips under his again and she responded with such vigour that it took them some time to realize the door of the hen-house had mysteriously swung open and their performance was being watched with interest by several beady-eyed hens.

'What a romantic setting,' said the viscount with

a laugh. 'Where is the dreadful Barry? I assume he locked us in deliberately.'

'Do not be angry. He always wanted me to marry you. Oh, dear, Papa is going to be so *mercenary*.'

'Nothing your family can say or do can worry me now.' He put an arm about her waist and she leaned her head on his shoulder and together they walked out of the hen-house.

The former Mary Stoppard, now Mary Judd, looked bleakly out at the gathering dusk of the winter's evening and was thankful her husband had gone off to London and she did not know when he was expected back. Being mistress of Mannerling was not what she had dreamt of, not what she had expected.

Also, her relationship with Mrs Judd had turned sour. Mrs Judd blamed her for her son's absence, saying if Mary were a proper wife, she would be able to keep him at home. She also blamed Mary for their lack of callers, sighing and moaning like the winter wind outside and saying that this was what came of 'poor Ajax' marrying beneath him.

Mary had been used to occupying her time with parish calls and gossip. But in her new position as mistress of Mannerling, she considered herself too grand to call on her old humble friends, and yet when she went calling on any important members of the county, she was always told they were 'not at home.' Snubbed and rejected, she blamed the Beverleys and thirsted for revenge. She felt sure it was they who had alienated the great and the good from visiting Mannerling.

Then her father, her very own father, had begun to compare her unfavourably to Isabella. 'If you had some of her air and elegance, my dear,' he would say sadly, 'then you would be more of a social success.'

On the outside of it, therefore, there was much to be pitied about Mary. But the hard core of devious selfishness and self-interest inside her kept her protected in a way. Nothing was or had ever been Mary's fault. There was always something or someone to blame. And Mannerling itself was a great comfort. She thought of it as hers, rather than her husband's, feeling the great house enfolding her, protecting her, calling her its own.

She had been on another search for the Beverley jewelry. How often had she imagined herself wearing some of those sparkling gems, seeing the Beverleys at a ball or party recognizing what had once been theirs and being as jealous of her as she had always been of them. So she wandered from room to room, under the ornate cornices and painted ceilings, looking, always looking. Mrs Judd had retired early for the night and so, apart from the odd servant going about his or her duties, she and the house were alone together.

And then she heard shouts outside and the sound of horses and carriage wheels. She ran to the window and looked down. Her husband was arriving with travelling carriage and outriders. The outriders extinguished their flaming torches, footmen rushed out to help the master down, John in the forefront, who had become the most obsequious of servants in case Mr Judd should ever change his mind and build that ruin and need a hermit.

Mary went down to the hall. She was determined to ask him about those jewels, but when he strode into the hall and she saw his glittering eyes and noted the unsteady way he walked, she gathered he was the worse for drink. So she tripped forward and kissed him on the cheek.

'Have you dined?' she asked.

'I don't need food and I don't need you,' he said curtly. He turned to the butler. 'Fetch me the brandy decanter and bring it to the library and then leave me.' He turned to Mary. 'Go to bed, Mrs Judd, for your Friday face is the last thing I want to see.'

Furious at the insult, Mary nonetheless went back upstairs, planning to attack him in the morning when he was fragile and sober.

Mr Judd went into the library and slumped down in an armchair and slung his muddy boots onto a footstool. A footman came in and added logs to the fire, another brought in the brandy and a glass, supervised by the butler.

'All of you go to bed,' he barked, 'and don't let me see your faces this night. Stay. What's that ladder doing in the hall?'

'We are cleaning the chandelier, sir. I will have it removed.'

'Leave it and leave me.'

Mr Judd sat in front of the fire and drank steadily. From time to time he sighed and looked about him.

Then he rose and made his way unsteadily to the window and jerked back the curtains.

Snow was beginning to fall, great white flakes drifting down from the night sky, swirling and rising and falling hypnotically.

All at once his brain felt miraculously clear, cold, and logical. He knew what he had to do.

Mary's first waking thought was about the jewels. She reached a hand out to summon the maid but then her eye fell on the clock and she groaned. It was only six in the morning. Mary would not admit to herself that she was cowed by the Mannerling servants. The bedroom was cold. She rose, shivering, and raked the fire, threw on some kindling from the basket beside the grate, lit it and waited, hugging her chest until the flames started rising up the chimney. She pulled back the curtains. Snow lay everywhere under the still dark sky, and snow was falling steadily. There was no sound at all. The whole countryside was wrapped in a blanket of winter silence.

She dressed hurriedly, thinking of several places in the house where she had not yet looked for the jewels. That great Chinese vase in the hall. Now *that* was the very place where her secretive husband might have hidden some of them.

All her worries forgotten, she made her way along the corridor from her apartment and down the stairs. Then, as she approached the main landing outside the chain of saloons, she realized that the silence was not absolute. There was a steady tinkling sound. Her face cleared. Some lazy servant must have left the main door open and the crystals in the great chandelier in the hall were tinkling in the draught.

She leaned on the banister and looked.

The chandelier with its Waterford crystals like white ice was just below her eye level. It was swinging gently because of a burden hanging from it. The long ladder lay on its side on the black and white tiles of the floor.

As she stared, the chandelier slowly swung round and the grinning, dead, purple, hanged face of her husband looked up at her and then slowly swung away again.

Mary's screams rent the great house from end to end. Up to the painted ceilings they went, past the family portraits in the Long Gallery, down to the servants' hall, where the sleepy chef started from his bed in the corner. It seemed they rushed out of the house, past the temple across the thin skin of ice on the ornamental lake and out over the fields.

Over in Perival, Mrs Kennedy woke shivering. She thought she had heard a banshee. She climbed stiffly down from her high bed and went to the window. But there was nothing outside but snow and more snow and the frozen silence of winter.

By rights Mr Judd, as a suicide, should have been buried at the crossroads with a stake through his heart to stop his ghost walking, but Mr Stoppard, the vicar, cried out that the owner of Mannerling should be buried in the churchyard and maintained the fiction that he had died of an apoplexy.

The funeral was barely over when the lawyers and duns began to gather like carrion crows at Mannerling. Slowly the news spread out across the countryside. Mr Judd had gambled everything away. Mannerling and its contents must be sold to pay the debts.

Isabella, despite her vow never to see Mannerling again, insisted that she and her sisters should call on Mary after the funeral and offer help and sympathy. But Mary sat there like a wounded animal surveying her with eyes full of such malevolence that Isabella wished she had not come.

She was too wrapped up in her own happiness, too much looking forward to her own wedding, to the next kiss and caress to realize the effect the news of the ruin and death of Mr Judd would have on her family. She did not guess that the viscount knew what to expect and was prepared for it.

Lizzie, who had returned to Brookfield House, nonetheless seized every opportunity to visit Perival and gladly agreed to accompany Isabella on a call, an Isabella who no longer sent Barry with a letter to announce her arrival, for a carriage from Perival arrived almost every day for her.

They were sitting in the drawing room with Mrs Kennedy and the viscount when they heard the arrival of a carriage. Lizzie ran to the window and looked out.

'It is Papa and the family,' she cried. 'What has caused them to hire a carriage and come calling when they could easily have come with us?'

Isabella's eyes flew to the viscount. He was looking grim.

'This is not going to be very pleasant for you, my dear,' he said to Isabella. 'Would you like to retire?'

'No,' she said, 'anything my family has to say to you is for my ears as well.'

'As you will. But it may distress you.'

Sir William and his family were ushered in. Isabella noticed with a feeling of dread that her father was looking gleeful, animated, and he was rubbing his hands.

After the initial pleasantries were over and everyone had been served with hot punch, Sir William leaned back in his chair and said expansively, 'Our Isabella is a lucky girl.'

'Thank you,' said the viscount. 'But I consider myself the most fortunate of men.'

'Aye, think what would have happened had she married Judd, which is what we hoped at one time she would do.'

Isabella winced.

'Ruined and hanged, hey? Mannerling to be sold and Mary to return to the vicarage. Sad.'

Sir William looked anything but sad.

'I am glad to see you,' said the viscount evenly, 'but is there any special reason for this visit?'

'No, no,' said Sir William hurriedly. 'Just a friendly call on my future son-in-law.' He looked about him. 'Tidy property you have here.'

'You have already remarked on it,' said the viscount.

Sir William leaned forward. Isabella studied her sisters, who all looked away, with the exception of Lizzie,

175

who was looking as puzzled and apprehensive as she was herself.

'It's not very *big*, though,' went on Sir William. 'I mean, you'll soon be married and setting up your nursery, and as Isabella is a healthy girl, bound to have lots of children, hey?'

'I also possess a comfortable home and estates in Ireland,' said the viscount, 'to which Isabella and I will be travelling immediately after the wedding.'

'Yes, yes, very fine, I'm sure, but both estates together cannot match Mannerling, and now it's up for sale—'

'Papa!' wailed Isabella, horrified.

'I am not buying Mannerling,' said the viscount. 'I will never buy Mannerling. I hope the place rots.'

Sir William bridled. 'It was only a suggestion. I thought if you loved Isabella, you would—'

But Isabella had leaped to her feet, her face flaming. 'How dare you humiliate me again, Papa. I never want to see Mannerling again. Oh, I went there to console Mary and that was a great mistake, but at least it showed me the madness of wanting the place. I suggest you all go home, please, before I lose my temper further.'

Lady Beverley began to cry softly with disappointment. 'You are a most unnatural daughter,' she sobbed.

Isabella stayed behind at Perival. The Beverleys, including Lizzie, sat sulkily in the carriage. When the gates of Mannerling came in sight, Sir William said suddenly, 'We should call on Mary. She is to move

176

to the vicarage soon. Only polite to offer help and sympathy.'

And so the Beverleys, who all detested Mary, pinned smiles of sympathy on their faces as the rented carriage drew up outside their old home.

Mary was savagely glad to see them, for ruined she might be, about to be banished to the vicarage she might be, but she knew it caused the Beverleys grief to see her still acting as mistress of Mannerling and ordering the servants around.

Sir William, finally ignoring Mary's digs about 'We are all poor now,' said, 'I suppose you have not yet found a buyer for Mannerling.'

'Oh, I have. A Mr and Mrs Devers of the Cornish family. Vastly rich, I believe.' Sir William's face fell.

'Any family?' asked Jessica suddenly.

'There is a son, I believe, Harry.'

'Will he be residing at Mannerling, too, with his wife?'

'He is not married. Late twenties, I believe.'

Mary bent over the tea-table and therefore did not see the darting little looks exchanged between the Beverleys.

Jessica let out a long sigh. All was not lost. An unmarried son! Well, she would succeed where Isabella, that fallen angel, had so miserably failed.

When they finally left, Lizzie trailed one slim hand along the mahogany banister. She had persuaded Mrs Kennedy and Isabella that she had been in the grip of a temporary madness, that never again would she even think about her old home. But she covertly studied

Jessica, noticing her elder sister's beauty. Jessica was made of steel, Jessica had all the determination and spirit which Isabella lacked, Jessica would never let mawkish love come between her and Isabella. Lizzie felt happier than she had felt for some time.

Isabella longed for her wedding day. She had not heard anything about the new owners of Mannerling and therefore could not understand the cheerfulness of the other members of her family. She could not put it down to an acceptance of their new life, for her sisters always seemed to be huddled together talking intensely and then, when they saw her, they would suddenly stop talking.

'They're plotting something,' she said to Barry one day, a Barry who had been more than forgiven for locking her in the hen-house with the viscount.

'Perhaps it's something to do with the new owners of Mannerling.'

'I knew it had been sold. Who are the owners, Barry?'

'A Mr and Mrs Devers. Accounted to be very rich. Old Cornish family.'

'Well, my father can hardly hope for one of my sisters to marry Mr Devers unless he plans to murder Mrs Devers.'

Barry leaned on the long axe he had been using to chop logs. 'There is a son, miss, a Mr Harry Devers, unwed, twenty-eight.'

'Oh, dear, what am I to do? The fools! They will humiliate themselves all over again.'

'May I say, miss, it is nothing to do with you. You will soon be going to Ireland and you will be well out of it.'

'How long will this madness last, Barry? Can you write?'

'Yes, miss, I have a fair hand.'

'Would you write to me from time to time to let me know how they go on?'

'Gladly, miss, though perhaps it might be better not to know.'

'Oh, I may be able to save them from their folly yet.'

The scullery boy came running over to tell Isabella that the carriage from Perival had arrived for her.

'I must go,' said Isabella. 'Thank you for everything, Barry.' She suddenly leaned forward and kissed him on the cheek.

Barry stood for a long time after she had left with a smile on his face.

Upstairs, Jessica turned away from the window. 'Isabella just kissed a *servant*. Ugh! The sooner I get the rest of you back to Mannerling, the better for you, or you might start kissing servants as well!'

Isabella alighted at Perival with a glad feeling of coming home. The viscount came out to meet her. 'Come in here,' he said, pulling her into a small morning room. He took off her bonnet and threw it on a chair and then fell to kissing her breathless.

'Oh, dear,' she said when she could. 'My dreadful family. You will never guess what they are plotting next.'

'The Devers have a son, a marriageable son, am I right?'

'Are they so transparent then?'

'Very.'

'What should I do?'

'Kiss me again.'

After a long time, he said huskily, 'Let your family learn by their mistakes, as learn they must. At least one brand has been saved from the burning. Little Lizzie has come to her senses.'

'Yes, I think Lizzie will grow into a fine woman. *She* will be as happy as I am now. I know it.'

He wound his arms tightly about her and would have spent the rest of the day in her arms had not Mrs Kennedy come in search of them and told them in forthright terms that it was customary to leave that sort of thing for the wedding night.

Barry carefully raked dead leaves and debris and then lit a bonfire and watched the flames and smoke crackle up into the clear frosty air.

And then he saw Lizzie, sitting on a fallen log at the far end of the garden. She was smiling all around. Her busy little hands served imaginary tea and offered imaginary cakes. Her mouth moved in soundless conversation.

Barry's heart smote him. All at once he was sure that Lizzie was dreaming herself back at Mannerling, acting as hostess. He felt he should tell Isabella, but Isabella would only fret.

He had been considering asking the viscount for a

post so that he might travel with them to Ireland. But he could better serve Isabella by staying where he was and trying to see that none of them came to any harm.

He stirred the bonfire impatiently.

And through the smoke he saw the imaginary mistress of Mannerling, still bowing and smiling and serving tea.